LOSING HOME

But Never Losing Hope

Joel Beeson

Cover Design by Robin Locke Monda

Book Design by Robert Henry at Right Hand Publishing

Published by Hawley House Publishing

ISBN: 979-8-9864057-1-1

This book is dedicated to the precious loved ones that inspire me to be a better man. My loving wife, Terry Beeson, has been by my side for fifty-one years, modeling the perfect helpmate that every man needs. My talented daughter, Nicole Mayfield, has inspired me to be the best person I can be as I observe the way she consistently demonstrates how she lays down her life for others. To a personal hero of mine, my son-in-law, John Mayfield, who easily masters and achieves all of his incredible personal goals. Finally, to my three terrific grandchildren, Claire Mayfield, Jacob Mayfield, and Bella Mayfield, who are wonderful people who have accomplished so much and will continue to achieve greatness in every aspect of their choosing.

CONTENTS

CHAPTER 1

The Old Country

John Delaney had finished most of his chores and he was now inventing errands outside the cottage. He wasn't sure what to do with himself as his mother alternated between moans and screams. This would be her seventh child and Molly was having more trouble with this delivery than she'd had with the others. Sean, the third oldest boy, had left a few hours before to fetch their father. The local midwife who was to preside over the birth was frail and elderly and she had a bad eye. It was glassy and it didn't track properly, wandering aimlessly as she spoke. John shuddered inwardly when she looked at him.

The cottage was small for a family their size, but it was temporary, deep in the western mountains, away from British eyes and influence. The Delaney family had left their ancestral home outside Galway months before. Michael Delaney, John's father, was known as Mickey. A leader among the Irish rebels, he was active in the resistance. The British had not yet tamed this region and the Delaneys were doing their part to ensure they never would. The rebels were more effective working from the hills, away from the cities the Brits controlled. The hills were their stronghold and from here they launched their most effective missions.

At ten, John's sister Nelly was the youngest, and as the only girl, she was accorded princess status in the family. She played with a field mouse scurrying between its nest and a small pile of grain as she waited for the baby to be born. She and John were close not only in age—he was three years older—but because they shared a special bond. John was her champion, her protector, and her best friend.

Abruptly, the screams of their mother ceased, replaced by the plaintive wails of a newborn.

"You have another sister," the midwife called out in Gaelic through the open window.

"Nelly, the baby is here," John shouted to his sister. "It's a girl."

Nelly scrambled up onto the steps, her face wreathed in smiles. Now she was not the only girl. She clapped and jumped up and down. Nelly was a passionate child and John always knew what she was thinking. Her emotions were like waves crashing on the nearby rocky beach.

John was the opposite. Few people knew what he was thinking or feeling.

"A girl! A girl! Let's go see her."

Before John could stop her, Nelly rushed into the house, straight to her mother's bedside. Molly was holding the baby. When she showed Nelly her tiny sister, the girl was overjoyed. John peeked in cautiously, unsure whether he should enter this most female of sanctums.

"Come see your sister, John," Molly said.

Molly thanked the midwife in Gaelic after the woman had tended to all the most pressing needs of mother and baby. John understood Gaelic. They all did, though they spoke mostly English. Molly demanded they speak the language of the market, as she called it, although most of the rural folk in the mountains still spoke the old language.

The midwife made a peculiar gesture with her hands—some sort of ancient blessing, John thought—then gathered her things and left.

John leaned over to see the baby.

"Sean has gone to find Paw," he said.

Molly nodded and handed the infant to John. He looked at this new sister for the first time. She had a reddish complexion and her dark eyes were only slightly opened. He thought he had never seen anything more perfect.

"I want to hold her!"

Molly smiled at her impatient daughter.

"In a minute darling. Your brother must hold her now. There will be plenty of opportunities for you. I am expecting you to oversee her most of the time, you know."

It was a family custom for an older sibling to be given charge of a younger one. Again, Nelly began jumping and clapping. As soon as she settled down, John handed her the baby.

It was late into the evening before their father and brothers returned.

"Mickey, the Lord has blessed us with another girl," Molly said, as she greeted her husband.

She was nursing the baby when he entered.

"Let's have a look at her, I bet she will be as pretty as her mother."

Mickey Delaney loved his family.

"Let her finish eating, we both have had a long day," Molly said.

Mickey stood over them both with pride only a new father can know. After a few moments, he went outside to clean up as the brothers filed into the house one at a time to see their new sister. Molly chatted with each of them about the new baby. Nelly remained resolutely at her mother's side. She wanted all to know this baby was to be her responsibility.

It was summertime, and the weather was mild. Mickey and the boys had a fire going out back. They were eating cold mutton on bread and talking about the day. When the baby was asleep, Molly sent Nelly to fetch Mickey.

"Mam wants you," she said.

Mickey finished the story he was telling, unhurried. It was a subtle way to let the family know he was not to be ordered around by a woman. Mickey knew a leader had to always be in control, even in his own home. He wanted to rush in and hug his wife, yet he had to always show strength to his sons. He strolled over to the cottage when he was ready.

"Sean, go and put Nelly to bed," said Michael, the eldest son.

The brothers knew the adults were to be left alone with the new baby.

Michael was not as tall as Mickey, but he had a sturdy build. He was a powerful man and a natural leader, and he had been trained by the best. No one questioned his authority. In a close-knit family like the Delaneys, though they challenged each other daily, the pecking order was clear. Michael was the alpha wolf. At twenty-two years old, he was a respected figure in the entire region. He often took charge of the forces as they fought together.

Behind the cottage was a smaller building the family was using as an overflow sleeping area. Sean did as his brother had asked. He didn't mind. He loved his sister, and she loved him. He usually told her stories as he tucked her into bed—stories about wizards, magic, and giants. John was her favorite brother, but Sean was a close second.

"How did it go today?" John asked when Nelly was out of earshot.

"Paddy almost got us all killed," Daniel said.

"Shut up. I did not."

"Paddy decided to sing us a tune at the top of his lungs when the Tans were a stone's throw away from us."

Tan was a slang term the Irish used to refer to the British soldiers in their khaki uniforms.

"We had no idea they were close to us," Patrick said.

"Well, they couldn't help knowing we were there. We were lucky they thought his singing was a cow trying to give birth," Daniel teased.

"It went well, John," Michael said in a low voice, treating his youngest brother not as a child but as the warrior he knew John would become.

"It was only a scouting party of five Tans snooping around. They will not be returning with a report, and we gained five good mounts, some much-needed ammunition, and eight nice rifles. It was a good day all around. As we were picking them clean and hiding the bodies, Sean found us, so we hurried back. In the morning we will need to finish what we started."

The boys had been organizing the volunteers in the area and scheduling upcoming activities for the next few weeks when they stumbled upon the British soldiers. They knew they would need to be more cautious in the future. They had been fortunate today. They chatted a bit more before they found a place to settle in and rest for the night. Tomorrow would be another busy day.

"You always look your prettiest when you hold one of our babies," Mickey said, as he gazed down at his wife and new daughter.

"Mickey, we are getting too old for this life."

They were alone now so it was safe to talk frankly with her husband. Their marriage had always been solid although they were both strong-willed. Molly was the kind of woman who spoke her mind freely.

"This is no way to raise a family," she added.

"We have done well so far."

"We had boys. It was easy to run from place to place with boys. They see it all as an adventure, a game. It's different with girls. I'll not be dragging young ladies all over these mountains, Mickey. It is time you let others do this nasty work. You have done enough."

"Did I miss something? Are the British gone?"

"They will never be gone," Molly replied. "You know that."

"What do you want me to do? Simply stop? Then what? What will the Brits do when we stop opposing them? You know what they will do."

It was a familiar argument they were having.

"Don't give me one of your patriotic speeches. I don't need this right now. I need us to take our rightful place where we belong."

Molly was talking about returning to Galway. The Delaney family owned a large estate east of the city. The lush pastureland would sustain them. They'd had a good life there until Mickey and his band of faithful warriors took to the hills.

Mickey had charge of a hundred good men scattered all through the mountainous region, each living his life as if nothing were wrong until called upon to carry out a raid, or whatever Mickey decided needed to be done. Their goal was to make life so miserable for the English that they would return to England and leave the Irish alone.

Molly knew Mickey would never give in and become British. And Mickey knew Molly would never stop wanting her family to be at peace. She knew they needed roots. They needed the church. They needed to be educated. All the boys were learning was war.

The two of them went back and forth a bit longer without deciding anything. Finally, they snuggled in silence, enjoying each other until they fell asleep.

The Crown had its eyes on the lush pastures of Western Ireland. Almost twenty percent of the population had either died of starvation or moved away during the potato famine. The Irish were now easy pickings for the English aristocracy. Queen Victoria was an accomplished monarch. Her hand-picked courtiers were capable, ambitious men and she was eager to rule the world. India, most of the trade routes to Asia, and a great portion of Africa were under her flag. England was the wealthiest nation since the Roman Empire centuries before. However, right up under her nose, the pesky Irish peasants would not submit to her God-given authority.

The English were becoming frustrated. According to many in Parliament, the Irish should be more civil and should accept their British lords. Some felt the backward Irish were slow learners. The Earl of Devon, a nobleman charged with taming the Irish, had recently appointed Sir Robert Peel to establish order in Western Ireland. Northern and Eastern Ireland were slowly becoming civilized. There were still the usual spats between the Catholics and the Protestants but for the most part, they behaved. The rebels in the West were considered an unruly lot, so Peel sent in battalions of police and soldiers to maintain order. The Irish called them Peelers. They were a rough bunch. Many of them had been part of the effort to tame India and they were a battle-hardened force. Things were about to become serious and Mickey and his boys knew it.

Mickey woke before Molly did. He was sitting in the corner holding his daughter when he saw his wife open her eyes. He smiled at her.

"What is her name?"

"I like Elizabeth Mary Delaney."

"That's a fine name."

He repeated the name a few times, gazing down at his child as he spoke.

"Yes, it's is a very fine name," he said.

Molly sat up in bed and motioned for him to bring her the baby. It had been several hours since the child had eaten, and Molly could feel her breasts becoming full. Michael gently handed the baby to his wife and stood over them as she nursed the child. When the infant finally fell asleep, he put a finger to his lips, smiled, and quietly backed out of the room. He needed to meet with his sons.

He smiled to himself as he watched them preparing for the day.

"Paw, you should stay here with Mam for a few days. We can handle this," Michael said.

"All right. Take John with you. But keep him close. Patrick can stay here with us. It would do him some good to be off the road for a few days"

He could tell his second oldest son was growing weary of this life. It was hard, and not everyone was cut out to be a warrior.

Mickey's confidence in Michael, his firstborn, had been forged over many missions, but this was the first time Michael had been given full responsibility. Their plan was straightforward, but Michael knew better than to take anything for granted.

"Daniel, I want you, John, and Malcolm to arrange for the transport of supplies to the designated location. You'll need to think through the practical aspects of the plan as you organize the work—and be alert to unexpected threats. We'll meet you at the drop site day after tomorrow—and we'll have the full crew, so be ready to launch."

John was excited to be with his brothers. It was not the first time he had gone with them, but this was different. They expected him to be a man, now—ready to do a man's job.

By nightfall, the wagons were loaded and everything was accounted for. Daniel and Malcolm had often worked together, but this was their first time to have John along.

"You did a man's work today, John," Daniel said. "I'm glad to have you with us."

John wasn't always sure how to take a compliment, but he grinned at his brother.

"Hey, don't get cocky," Daniel said, throwing his arm over John's shoulder. "Get some sleep. We've got a big day ahead, and I don't want you to slow us down."

Early the following day, they set out on what should have been a six-hour trip through rough country. They were gone about an hour when Malcolm spotted a single rider off their left flank. Before they could agree on what should be done, John peeled off.

"Keep the horses moving, I'll go see what it is," he said, as he galloped off.

Malcolm arched an eyebrow but Daniel nodded. Both Mickey and Michael had commented on John's instincts and Daniel trusted his little brother.

John's quarry had no idea he had been seen. Nor did he see the caravan. John fell in behind the man and followed at a safe distance. After getting a closer look, he identified the man as a British soldier in the usual khaki uniform. John drew closer, watching. After a while, the man stopped and got off his horse. He did not appear to be in any real hurry.

John approached the soldier on foot. The man had stopped to stretch his legs and empty his bladder. He was busy fastening the buttons on his trousers as John stepped out from behind some rocks with his long gun pointed at the soldier.

"Hold it, son," the man said. "Now, put the gun down."

John cocked the hammer.

"I am a member of Her Majesty's Police. If you don't lower your weapon, I will have to arrest you."

John moved in quickly, catching the man off guard. He shoved the barrel of his gun into the man's mid-section, driving all the air from his lungs. The soldier fell to his knees.

"Sit down," John said.

The man flopped backward, gasping for breath. John found a leather strap used to tie the man's gear to his horse. He bound the man's hands behind his back. Once the fellow was secured, John went through his belongings. He found the usual things a policeman would have. The only thing out of the ordinary was a satchel filled with papers. John could not read so he had no idea what they were.

John tied up his prisoner behind his horse, then walked the man across the rocky stretch to where he figured he would find Malcolm and Daniel. He saw them about the time they reached the canyon. Daniel secured the prisoner as John filled them in on the capture. John and Malcolm unloaded the supplies and tended to the horses as Daniel looked through the satchel. It was almost dark when Michael and Sean arrived with a dozen men. Daniel told Michael the story.

"John, come with me," Michael said, later in the evening.

Michael had spent the last few hours talking with the soldier, who was in no mood to resist after being dragged by a rope over rough country for half the day. John was not sure if he was in trouble for riding off after the man.

"What made you go after the rider?" Michael asked.

"Something didn't feel right."

His big brother looked at him for a long time.

"Well as it turned out, John, my boy, it was a stroke of luck. What we learned from the documents and what the man reported was most helpful. It changes everything for us. And for the better."

He put his arm around the boy.

"I'm proud of you. But don't tell Mam what you did. She will skin us both."

The intelligence they had gained from the prisoner led to a change of plans. Early the next morning, most of the men stayed with the supplies while Malcolm and the Delaney boys hurried to the cottage to talk with Mickey. The prisoner was of no further use to them. He could not be released because he knew where their supplies were being held, so his throat was cut and his body was buried on the far side of the mountain, never to be found.

In their absence, Mickey had had time to reflect on what his wife had said. He always listened to her because he loved her and knew she had his best interest at heart. He'd been able to put the resistance out of his mind and concentrate on his girls for a couple of days and this did him good. He played and laughed with Nelly. He held Elizabeth. He and Molly went for long walks, laughing and talking and enjoying each other. He and Patrick worked around the cottage repairing fences and tending to animals. Before the boys returned, Mickey had decided what the family would do. Mickey loved Ireland, but he loved his family more. It was becoming clear he could not have both.

When the boys arrived, they found Mickey playing with Nelly. While the rest of the brothers settled in, Mickey and Michael walked off together. John kept an eye on them. Father and eldest son talked seriously for almost an hour, which was odd because both men were known to be direct, wasting no words with long drawn-out conversations. When they finished, Mickey gathered the entire clan together.

"Your mother and I have decided we need a change. The time is right for Michael to take over the business."

They all knew what he was talking about. The family business was opposing the British Crown.

"Patrick and Finnegan will leave in the morning for Sunrise Estates," Mickey said.

Their ancestral home sat in a pretty valley. It glowed when the morning sun peeked over the mountains to the east. The moist breeze off the Atlantic was perfect for growing tall grass to keep their sheep fat. Finnegan O'Toole, Molly's uncle, was an old warrior who had followed Mickey for years. He had spent time in a British prison while the greedy English carved up his land and destroyed his family. Mickey knew he would be the perfect man to work with Patrick in restoring the family's home.

"Patrick and Finnegan will set things in order, purchase sheep and get the operation going. The girls and I will join them in the fall. You boys can choose the life you want. If you decide to work in the business, you will follow Michael as you have followed me. If you decide to join us at Sunrise Estates, you will live and work there as long as you wish.

Tomorrow, we will leave by noon. It will be my last run with you so let's make it a run to remember."

CHAPTER 2

Galway, Ireland

William Conway was what polite society referred to as a "troubled youth". If his father had not been an important member of the Royal Police Force, the boy would have been classified as a common criminal. Young William had been recently expelled from a prestigious school in Dorset. The Conways had attended Craneborne for generations. Quite a scandal had ensued when young William and a couple of his friends were caught in the act of breaking into the headmaster's office and making off with his best whiskey. If it had been anyone else, jail time would have been required, but the whole matter was handled discreetly since his father was Sir Thomas Conway.

William's mother had decided she could no longer deal with him, so he had been shipped off to Western Ireland to live with his father, who had recently been appointed Provincial Chief of Police. Matters like this can never be kept quiet, which meant most of the men under Conway knew all about the boy. Consequently, Chief Conway was not happy when his son arrived. They had never been close, but even if William had been a model son, it was still the worst possible time for him to show up in Galway.

"Watson, get in here," Conway yelled at his orderly.

He was crumpling up the new orders he had received and throwing them into the fireplace. Watson saw the official papers being burned and he knew this was highly irregular. Papers from the Crown were to be filed and kept in a secured place. He looked at his superior with a frightened expression.

"I want all my captains in this office first thing in the morning. No excuses and I mean every one of them. I do not care if they must travel all night to get here. I expect them all here and on time,"

"Yes sir."

He left the room briskly. Watson did not want to be around Chief Conway when his temper was high.

The letter, now only ashes in the fire, had been clear. The Crown was not pleased with Conway's job performance. Sir Robert Peel had given Conway a deadline. If the rebellion in his province was not under control by the end of the summer, Conway would be stripped of his position and relocated to some remote part of the world. The Queen was tired of being humiliated.

The following morning, Conway was finishing his breakfast, awaiting notice that his captains were assembled. He was rehearsing the speech he would give his men. He had been up most of the night planning how he would accomplish his goal of restoring order. As if he didn't have enough to worry about, young William had now walked into the dining room wearing only his undertrousers. His hair was unkempt and he had no shirt. William was a nice-looking young man with pleasant features and the chiseled body of an athlete. He was rather proud of his appearance. Sir Thomas, however, was not impressed. At seventeen years old, the young man was grown. He was two inches taller than his father and in much better shape physically. Thomas had been behind a desk for many years, so his physical condition was not what it had been. His anger erupted like a spewing volcano.

"I should think it proper to get dressed before you come downstairs.

Get out of my sight, you vulgar moron."

He threw the water glass he was drinking from at his son. It flew past the boy's head, smashing into a thousand pieces as it hit the wall.

"I have people coming here. How dare you walk around in my house in such a disgraceful fashion."

"I guess I'll have my breakfast in my room," William said, with a grin. He was not afraid of his father and he had no respect for him.

"Patel, bring my breakfast up," he ordered.

He smirked as he commanded the Indian man who stood at attention near his father. Patel had worked for the family for years. He knew all about William. Patel escorted the young man upstairs, but not before William scratched his posterior in an exaggerated fashion, simply to irritate his father further. Patel, speaking Hindi, ordered the kitchen maids to clean up the broken crystal.

Conway wanted to take a whip to the boy and lock him in the cellar for weeks. Maybe he would later, but for now, he had to get his mind back on his business. He was not in a pleasant mood when Watson appeared, announcing the meeting would be delayed at least a few hours. Captain Gant had not arrived. Gant was assigned to the wilderness. The wilderness was the least populated area, but also the area where most of the rebels were encamped. It was the most remote region with the most trouble. Gant was a good man. He was probably the only man capable of policing the area.

It was almost noon before the meeting began. William had not come out of his room. Patel was standing guard, making sure the two Conway men did not cross paths again. His men were standing at attention when Conway walked into his parlor. He did not allow them to be at ease. He began his practiced speech with the vigor of a polished politician.

"Every morning when you awaken, I want you to declare out loud, *'Whatever it takes.'* While you are shaving and getting dressed you are to say, 'Whatever it takes.' Before each meal, you will repeat, 'Whatever it takes.' All through the day, you should say, 'Whatever it takes.' The last thing I want you to be thinking about when you retire at night is 'Whatever it takes.' Can I make it any clearer?"

Sir Thomas was exaggerating every syllable. He paused, looking each captain in the eye.

"By the end of July, I want every single rebel and any Irish cur who dares even to think about rebellion either dead or in chains. I do not care what they are charged with. Make up a charge if you must. I will back you on it. Peel will back you on it. The Queen herself will back you if needed. I will visit each one of you regularly to evaluate your performance. No excuses. You are dismissed. Now start rounding them up immediately."

He left the room without another word. He was pleased with himself. The message had been delivered properly. It was only a matter of time now.

While Conway was planning the rebels' demise. the first group of Delaneys was emerging from the mountains on their way to Sunrise Estates. Patrick and Finnegan O'Toole had been weaving the loaded wagon through the mountain trails for two days. Springtime in Western Ireland is a lovely time of year and they were enjoying each other's company. Patrick liked the old man, who had plenty of wisdom to share from a rich background completely unknown to Patrick. Curious by nature, he wanted to know more about his mother's uncle, especially since they would be spending so much time together.

"Tell me, Finnegan," he said. "How does a refined gentleman like yourself end up running around with ruffians like the Delaneys?"

"Your father saved my life," he said, looking Patrick in the eye.

He went silent and looked at the horses' rumps as they proceeded.

"You can't leave it there. You need to tell me the story."

"It's a long story, but you are right. I can't leave it at that. Not with you anyway. You will continue to trouble me with questions until you are satisfied," O'Toole said with a smile.

"Go on, we have plenty of time," Patrick said.

O'Toole began his story. He had been a well-educated young man from an established Irish family. The English were toying with allowing the Irish to represent themselves in Parliament. Most of the lords sent to London from Ireland were British transplants, however, they allowed a few Irish members whom they thought they could control, at least for appearance's sake. They thought this young educated man was safe. So, O'Toole was allowed to represent Galway.

For a while, all went well, until the day he opposed an influential nobleman named Frances Cornwall. O'Toole forced a procedural vote. This caused the motion Cornwall was pushing to fail. It was an embarrassment Cornwall was not prepared to tolerate. O'Toole won the battle but it cost him dearly. He now had an influential—and furious—enemy.

A few weeks later, O'Toole was in court defending himself against the charge of threatening the Crown. In London, it was easy for a charge like this to be taken seriously when an Irishman was involved. He was found guilty. There were several classes of criminals. The worst were rapists, murderers, and those accused of treason. The usual sentence for this crime was either the gallows or transportable imprisonment. Since the British needed workers in Queensland, Australia, young Finnegan was loaded on a boat and shipped away before his family got word of what had happened to him.

Molly O'Toole was the niece of Finnegan and she was upset at his plight. She was engaged to marry Mickey Delaney, and when Mickey saw the pain this had caused his sweet Molly and learned how unjust the entire ordeal had been, he booked passage to Australia to see if he could correct this wrong. There was nothing he would not do to restore happiness to his beloved Molly. Personally opposing the Crown had already become a way of life for young Mickey Delaney.

It took Mickey some time to work out the details. Australians were no kinder to the Irish than the English were. But finally, after months of planning, he accomplished his goal.

O'Toole went into detail describing how harsh prison life had been. He was ready to end it all when one day, while he was working on a chain gang, Mickey Delaney showed up in a guard's uniform and escorted O'Toole out of the prison. They made their way to the eastern coastline where Mickey had booked passage, under assumed names, to Lisbon, Portugal. From there, they traveled by land through Spain to Balboa, where they boarded a ship bound for Galway.

Mickey Delaney was soon married to Molly. He was her hero after saving her beloved uncle. O'Toole spent the rest of his life avoiding the British and doing his part to rid Ireland of them. Mickey and Finnegan were as close as brothers.

The rest of the Delaneys were training and planning the attack they had scheduled. Young Michael took charge as Mickey continued to focus on his youngest son, John. He had already spent a considerable amount of time with John, who was now thirteen years old and was growing larger and stronger by the day. Both Mickey and Michael had been impressed by John's capture of the British courier, and John realized he was now being treated like the rest of the men. His father was teaching him to be a warrior. This meant you must win the fight, or you might not live to fight again. Over and over Mickey showed him how to attack his opponent.

"Be exact," Mickey would say. "Know what you are going to do before the fight. The fight is won by the man who knows what he wants to do."

John knew this meant to never let the other man choose. Always fight on your terms or do not fight.

"Never be distracted by your emotion. The time to deal with such things is after the battle," his father would say.

The day's attack was successful. The British were establishing an outpost not far from the hills the Irish were operating from. An hour before dawn, they burned the entire place down, destroying the British fort. Only a few men escaped on foot. It was anyone's guess as to whether any would make it back alive.

John did well in the fight. Mickey stayed close to him as his brother Michael led the men. The rest of the day and most of the next was spent gathering the livestock and plundering the refuge. John had survived his first major battle knowing there would be plenty more in the months ahead.

A few of the British soldiers did make it back and when word reached Conway, he was furious. His new directives became harsher than the previous orders. Irish blood was required to pay for this loss. The police raided the homes of those they suspected had either participated in the raid or knew about it. One home was Malcolm's. Of course, old Malcolm knew all about it. He had been beside young Michael the entire time. He was taken in for questioning. The beatings he received for not talking were severe enough to cause his death. When word got back to the Delaneys, Michael's blood boiled. It was personal now. An eye for an eye. The Tans would pay dearly for this outrage. The Irish patriots immediately moved from harassing the British to hunting them. Michael's orders were clear. For every Irishman they lost, the British would pay with five. The word went out across the land. *Five for one* became their motto.

By the time Mickey, Molly, and the girls left for Galway, Western Ireland was in an all-out war. Conway was doing his best to replenish his troops but he was losing ground. His men were ready to revolt and were refusing to go into the hills without more troops and proper support. The Tans who went into the mountains on recon often were never seen again. Every time they thought they had an opportunity to confront the Irish scallywags, the Irish simply vanished before they could be engaged. The usual tactics, like making an example of the criminals, were useless. The Irish were more ruthless than they should have been and the British were losing more men than they were able to capture. Moreover, the number of rebels was growing. The resistance was becoming fashionable. The British were not prepared for this type of war. For a short time, young Michael Delaney and his band of raiders proved more effective than the mighty British Empire.

Mickey managed to stay away from it for the most part, as he struggled to keep his word to Molly. Soon they would be settled into their home, where the girls could be raised properly. Molly had never been happier. Elizabeth was a beautiful, healthy baby and Nellie and her father had grown close over the months.

In late summer, Patrick went to Galway by himself to attend a sheep auction. They had restored the living area, repaired the barns, and planted a garden. He and his uncle Finnegan were making progress. Going into Galway was a job Patrick had to do by himself since his uncle stayed away from populated areas where the British were known to be. O'Toole would go into Currow, the small town nearby because there were no Brits there. Galway was different. The population of Galway in 1850 was almost ten thousand people. It had been over fifteen thousand before the potato famine reached its peak in 1845. In Galway, there were nearly 2500 non-Catholics—the largest number of Anglicans in Western Ireland. This meant they were most likely British or British sympathizers. Finnegan knew not to venture close to the area. Patrick must handle this task alone.

After purchasing a flock of young sheep, he arranged for help to move them north. As he loaded supplies into his wagon, he spotted the most beautiful girl he had ever seen. Her amber hair curled naturally, flowing off her elegant shoulders. Bright, sparkling blue eyes highlighted a pretty face that transfixed Patrick where he stood as she entered the store. She moved with the graceful elegance of a lady. Patrick dropped the sack he was holding and jumped off the wagon. He had no reason to go back into the store, but he did so without thinking. He was drawn to this angelic creature.

As he came through the door he froze once more when she turned to look at him. She had a puzzled expression on her face.

"Sir," Patrick said to the merchant. "I need to purchase another box of nails."

"They are over there," the bald man behind the counter said. "The same place they were ten minutes ago."

This embarrassed Patrick but it made the young lady smile. Patrick stared at her again. The embarrassment was a small price to pay for such a smile. He walked past her to get the nails and she nodded at him, still smiling. He nodded back. He realized she had made the first move. Maybe she liked him?

He paid for the nails, then went back to his task of loading the wagon, but not before he glanced back at her. She was still smiling at him. A few minutes passed and she stepped out of the store, accompanied by an older lady. They had bundles of fabric. His father would have been furious at Patrick. He had been taught to know his surroundings, but he had no idea what was going on around him. He was captured by her beauty. This older lady had been with her the entire time and Patrick had not noticed her. Mickey Delaney had said many times to "never neglect to see what is there". The girl's beauty had blinded him. The old lady could have been an armed soldier and Patrick would not have noticed.

Before Patrick could straighten up, the older lady stepped forward holding out her hand for him to stop.

"You have no business talking with this girl," she said in Gaelic. "Get back to your own business right now."

Now what? Before he could figure out what to do the pretty girl spoke.

"My name is Lucinda Conway. With whom do I have the pleasure of speaking?"

"Lady Lucinda," the Irish lady said.

"It's quite all right," said the sweetest voice Patrick had ever heard.

It was an angel's voice. Then it hit him: a British angel, if there was such a thing.

"My name is Patrick Delaney."

She reached into her handbag and located a card, which she handed to Patrick.

"So pleased to meet you, Patrick Delaney."

On the card in bold letters was written the name "Wallace Conway," with an address. He was watching her walk away when he realized his life would never be the same. He knew he could not live without her. He was in love. In love with the enemy.

C H A P T E R 3

The Courtship

Over the next few weeks, Patrick thought of every possible reason to be in Galway. He could not stop calling at the address on the card. Lucinda Conway lived there with her father Wallace, an accountant for a shipping company. His job was to ensure the cargo on the ships came and went as expected. After becoming acquainted with her father, Patrick was not sure how he managed his duties as an accountant since he was rarely sober. Perhaps he was drunk when he gave his consent to Patrick to call on his daughter. Being English, Wallace naturally thought he was superior to the Irish. He should have denied the young man access to her, but his parenting skills had long ago vanished from an overabundance of whisky.

"How could such a brutish race develop such a refined drink," he often said, when opening a fresh bottle of Irish whisky.

At first, Patrick had gone once a week; now he was going every other day. He would bring her fresh flowers or some other token. He also brought a bottle or two of whiskey for Wallace to keep him busy. Lucy, as he was calling her, was growing fond of him as well. This was Patrick's plan. He was already deeply in love with her, and the more they got to know each other, the more his love grew.

Molly could not stop smiling as they arrived in the valley. It had been years since she had seen her precious Sunrise Estates. The place still needed work, but it was obvious Patrick had done a good job getting things ready. He had hired several local men to help. The Delaneys had money, though much of it had been taken from the Tans. When Patrick and Finnegan arrived with cash, the local economy of this small community began to flourish. Finnegan was there to meet them as they arrived.

"Where is Patrick?" Molly inquired.

"Lately he has had a lot of business in Galway," he said, as he shot Mickey a glance.

"Help us get unloaded and we can catch up on things," Mickey said.

Finnegan called and a few men appeared from the barn to take care of the luggage.

Later, after they were all settled in, Finnegan and Mickey went for a walk. Finnegan told him all about Patrick's visits to Galway. Patrick had not said a word to Finnegan about what he had been doing so Finnegan had taken it upon himself to find out. He had arranged for Patrick to be followed.

Mickey, as expected, was not happy about Patrick seeing an English woman. What in the world had gotten into this boy? The two old friends talked about everything. Mickey brought him up to date on all happening in the hills and O'Toole went over what had been done and what was left to get done before winter. As the two men spoke, Nelly rocked her sister on the porch. She was taking her job as the baby's nanny seriously.

While they were talking, Patrick came riding up. He greeted his father and went in to see his mother. A few minutes later he joined the older men as they sat talking. Mickey was so upset about his son's courtship of an English girl, he'd decided it best that he didn't speak to him. Patrick could read his father's disapproval and he accepted his silence.

Mickey was telling Finnegan about the struggle. Michael was headquartered in the same cottage where Elizabeth had been born. He'd divided the force into three groups. He led a group of between fifty and sixty seasoned warriors. Another group was led by Sean, who had about thirty men—half were new and still being trained. The last group was located deep in the mountains where they kept their supplies. Daniel and John led this group of about twenty men. Most of them were young. Finnegan nodded as he listened. He approved of young Michael's choices.

Michael was aggressively taking the battle to the Brits. The raiders would alter their tactics and strategies to keep the English guessing. Sean had also become a solid leader. He was effective at training and his men respected him. In all the battles he had not yet lost a single man. His jovial nature was endearing to the men, and they had a good time as they brought hellfire down on the Brits.

Daniel and John worked together well. John was growing into an impressive warrior. Daniel made sure he learned caution to go with his fearless nature. Of all the boys, John and Michael were the fiercest fighters. Violence was in their blood.

Back in Galway, Thomas Conway was not happy with the results he was getting. It was clear they could not continue at this rate. The rebels were gaining strength. His men were making plenty of arrests but he suspected they were merely rounding up random citizens. Meanwhile, he was losing good men. As their conscriptions expired, many were choosing to leave. Western Ireland had become the hellhole of the British Empire. His correspondence with Peel had become vile. Blame was given and deflected as with two combatants locked in a deadly joust. His best chance of salvaging the situation was to amass a large army and take the fight to the mountains. If he had enough men, he could clean up the region. He was sure of it. Conway was leaving for London on the next ship. Peel would have to give him what he needed; there was no other way.

It had been several days since Patrick had visited and Lucy was worried. Her father was the happiest he had been in years. They were going to move into his cousin's house and run things while Thomas was in London. The London trip would take weeks and Wallace was looking forward to being master of the house. Thomas would take some servants with him, but there were plenty who would stay behind to prepare fine meals and pour Wallace's drinks for him. Wallace had grown up in this manner and he missed it. He had managed to lose his family endowment. Now he had to work a humiliating job like a commoner—in addition to sponging off the few relatives who would still speak with him. Thomas was one of the few who tolerated him.

Two days after Mickey and the girls arrived, Patrick and his father were still not speaking. Mickey was not going to accept Patrick's poor judgment. But Finnegan had now taken ill with a high fever. He refused to see a doctor because it meant going to Galway. He could not shake the fever and it got worse. The following day, after staying up half the night with him, Patrick and Mickey made a bed for him in the wagon and Patrick took him to Galway to see a doctor. By this time, Finnegan was too weak to object.

It was already dark in Galway and most businesses were closed. Patrick inquired until he found a doctor who would see Finnegan. The doctor decided he needed to be hospitalized immediately. Patrick arranged for the hospital to take him. He stayed up all night for the second night in a row, making sure Finnegan was taken care of properly. A couple of hours after dawn, Mickey arrived. He spoke his first words to his son, telling him to get some rest—now he would watch after Finnegan.

Patrick left the hospital but did not go home. He went to Lucy's house but he discovered they were gone. A note was posted with the forwarding address listed for any correspondence. Patrick found the address. It was a stately house owned by Sir Thomas Conway, Galway's police chief. He wanted to turn and leave, but he couldn't make himself do it. He knocked on the door, and when an Indian man answered the door, he inquired about Lucinda.

Patrick was pleased when the door opened, and Lucy stepped out. She smiled at him and escorted him into the house. Servants were watching as he and Lucinda walked down the long hallway to the library.

"I was hoping you would be able to find us."

"I have been finding out a lot lately," Patrick said.

"Like what?"

He looked around and saw several servants in the room with them. waiting for instructions. It made him uncomfortable.

"Is there somewhere we can talk alone?"

"Of course," she said.

She asked the servants to leave them as they stepped out into an adjoining garden. She led him to a shaded bench and they sat together.

"Isn't this nice?"

"Yes, it is."

"What is wrong?" she asked.

"When were you going to tell me you are kin to Thomas Conway?" Patrick demanded.

"What difference does it make who I'm kin to?"

Lucy was confused and getting a little upset with him.

"Do you have any idea who I am?" Patrick asked.

"Patrick Delaney is who you said you were. Are you not Patrick Delaney?

"I am. Do you know who the Delaneys are?" he asked.

"Only what you have told me. Remember, I am not from around here."

"Why are you interested in me?"

Patrick's tone was harsh.

"Are we quarreling?" she asked. "If we are, I'd like to think it's over something consequential; not this silliness."

"Why did you hand me your card the day we met?" he continued.

"Maybe I should not have. I had no idea you were stark raving mad. If you can't come to your senses soon, I may have to ask you to leave. This conversation is giving me a headache."

"You do not know about the Delaneys?" he asked.

"I've already answered."

"Swear to me you are telling the truth."

He gently held her shoulders and leaned in to look into her eyes.

Her voice quivered.

"I swear on my saintly mother's grave that before we met, I had never heard of you or your family. You are scaring me."

"You have never spoken of me to Thomas Conway?" Patrick continued.

"I have not spoken to Thomas since last Christmas. We have never been close. He is a busy man, and frankly, I don't care much for him. He is cruel to me and my father. I have no idea why we are forced to associate with him… oh, I take it back. I know why. It's because he controls the family trust."

"Let's take a walk," Patrick said.

They stood up and she allowed him to take her hand. They walked through the garden as he told her about his family—a clan of proud Irishmen who had always opposed British rule. They walked from garden to garden as he told his story. She also told him hers. She was non-political on every level. She did not care for politics of any kind. Neither did Wallace. She explained how her father had squandered his share of the fortune and now had to grovel at his cousin's feet to get by. It was a humiliating tale, but she told it. Patrick left there confused, but he knew he was still in love.

Mickey and Patrick alternated staying with Finnegan as he recovered. Mickey wouldn't leave him alone for fear Finnegan would walk once he realized he was in Galway. After three days in the hospital, he finally shook the fever. The doctors were not sure why he was ill. The best they could guess was some sort of blood disorder. He was released and Mickey wasted no time getting him out of Galway.

During the hospital stay, Mickey and Patrick had time to talk about Lucinda. Mickey believed Patrick when he said the love affair had been an innocent happenstance, but he still thought it foolish. He also trusted his son not to betray the family. But he told him if he continued seeing Lucy, he could have nothing to do with the family business. Patrick happily agreed. He was sick of the violence.

Patrick was not the only one with his eye on Lucy. Young William, her fourth cousin, had noticed how beautiful she was, and now that they were living under the same roof, he wanted to assert his claim. He had tried his best to gain her approval with his flirtatious jests, but she was not interested. She had ignored every gesture and this was beginning to anger him.

One day, William and a companion were at home enjoying whiskey with Lucinda's father. It was early afternoon, but Wallace had been drinking heavily and he was barely conscious. After he stumbled off to his room, the two boys continued drinking. Their conversation had turned coarse as they talked about their preferences at one of several brothels in the area.

When Lucy passed William and his friend on her way to the drawing room, William decided she was not going to be rude to him any longer. She had no right to be so uppity.

"Aren't you going to speak with our guest?" he asked, as she passed the parlor where they were lounging.

"Good afternoon, sir," she said with a nod, continuing toward the drawing room.

"Lucinda," William barked. "What gives you the right to be so curt to my guests? I should think it proper for you to stop and offer a bit more courtesy than your typical backstreet rude manners. I know you come from the gutter, but you do not need to always remind everyone of your commonness."

She ignored him and went on to the drawing room. This angered William as much as it amused his friend Ralph.

"I guess you showed her who was master," Ralph taunted him in a sarcastic voice. "You may be the cock of the walk at the brothel where your money pays for respect, but in your own home you are merely another chick pecking for bugs,"

Ralph knew he had hit a nerve. He took another swig of the whiskey.

"Has she ever even spoken to you?" he asked.

"Shut up."

CHAPTER 4

London

Parked on an overstuffed sofa outside Lord Peel's office, Thomas Conway felt like a schoolboy, summoned to the headmaster's office. It was his meeting. He had a plan to present. It was a good plan so why was he panicked? He knew if he did not win the day, he would be leaving his position in disgrace. At his age, he could not accept another assignment in India, Australia, or any other far-off land. He needed to fix this problem in Ireland and go out as a conqueror, not a failure. His pride would not allow him to walk away. He must win this last battle. Whatever it took. Peel should understand this. After all, it would make him look good as well. Peel surprised him by opening the large oak door himself.

"Thomas, my boy, why look at you. The ocean air is doing wonders for you. You look as fit as ever. Come in, come in."

"Sir," Conway nodded to his superior as they entered the large room.

Peel put his hand on the man's shoulder and ushered him deeper into his office. As soon as they were inside Peel barked a command to an adjacent room. From across the room, a uniformed attendant brought a service tray with tea and biscuits.

"Have a seat, Thomas, and tell me what is on your mind."

Peel was still speaking as if to a beloved nephew whom he'd not seen in years. Conway could not figure this out. They had never been close, though he had worked for the man off and on for many years.

"Your Lordship," he said, "The situation in my region is more serious than anyone suspected.

"Go on, I'm listening."

"The usual strategies for transforming these subjects into proper citizens is never going to work. They reject everything about us. They are more clannish than any people I've ever seen. I will tell you the truth: the medieval Islamists of Asia are easier to sway than these stubborn Irish."

"Please continue," Peel said, as he sipped his tea.

"I am afraid a more aggressive strategy will be required. I am convinced we must break their spirit before they will submit to authority," Conway said.

Peel thought for a moment. He frowned.

"Let me remind you of this: the Queen is watching us closely. The Empire has no desire to be bogged down in another quagmire like the one in the colonies. The Queen has made this clear. She has also made clear the fact that she will not continue to put up with the Irish insurrection. So, there we have it," Peel said.

Conway listened without betraying any emotion. He had to present his case now, despite the fact Peel had already made it clear he was not going to be given regular military troops.

"Scotland and Eastern Ireland are behaving quite nicely, why can't these people? For Christ's sake, they are of the same Celtic stock. What is the problem?" Peel asked.

"Sir, I am not here to discuss the subtle social differences between these Celts versus others we rule. Respectfully, I'm here to give you my assessment as well as a solution to this problem. We must put a boot on their throats until they feel it. I understand it needs to be done discreetly, but if we don't do it now, we will never gain control."

"What is your proposal?" Peel asked.

"We need to impose martial law," Conway replied.

He went on to lay out his plan for correcting the problem, and by the end of the meeting, Peel was on board. He would allow assets to be transferred and orders would be drawn up to put Conway's plan in place.

It didn't take long. A week later, in the mountains of Western Ireland, the day began as any other day, with Daniel and a man named Clincher patrolling the perimeters of the area. But suddenly a shot rang out. and a musket ball entered the back of Clincher's head, ruining his face completely as it exited. Clincher dropped from his horse like a rock. The shot spooked Daniel's horse and he bucked Daniel off, stepping on his rider's left leg above the ankle. Clincher's horse ran off as Daniel's steed continued to buck.

Daniel knew his leg was broken. He had heard it snap. He was in pain but he managed to get himself up on his good leg. As he reached his horse, he heard men coming up from behind him.

One grabbed him as he reached for his horse's bridle. Daniel turned and drove his long blade knife deep into the man's gut. The other soldier swung his rifle and the barrel of the weapon came down hard on the side of Daniel's head. It was the last thing he remembered.

John and the others heard the shot and knew something was wrong. Not long after the shot, Clincher's mount came running up, covered in blood. A lot of blood. They knew it wasn't the horse's.

John ordered the men to prepare for an attack. He knew it was coming. He climbed on the bloody horse and rode out, looking for his brother and Clincher.

Daniel finally came to late in the day. He'd been draped across his horse and his hands and feet were tied together under the horse's belly. He heard men talking as they made camp. After they had a fire going, one man came over and untied him from the horse, letting him drop to the ground like a sack of grain. He dragged Daniel over and tied him to a tree. Daniel never moved. He knew his leg was swollen without having to look at it. He needed time to think, but his head was throbbing from the blow.

He opened one eye to see only three men. The one Daniel had stabbed was in bad shape. He would probably die sometime in the night, he thought. Daniel knew to keep still. If they thought he was conscious the interrogation would begin. He was in too much pain to endure torture.

John found the location of the ambush in short order. Clincher's body lay where he had dropped. John could tell they had gone through his pockets looking for information. He had no doubt as to who was behind the attack.

As he looked around, two of his men arrived. One of them loaded Clincher onto his horse. The other took off to report the ambush to Michael. John knew from the tracks there were only a few of them—three or four at the most. He was worried about his brother so he wasted no time. He followed the trail until it got too dark. There was no moon and it was cloudy, so he settled in for the night. It was too dangerous to take a horse through this rough country in the dark. A few hours later, it started raining. John was mad at himself for not pushing on. He might lose their trail if it rained hard enough. It was a long night. When daylight finally came, John was so wet and cold he could barely feel his toes and fingers. He continued tracking the party.

The men returned to Daniel as soon as it was light enough to see. They began taking turns slapping him until they knew he was awake.

"What is your business here?" asked the older man.

"I live here," Daniel replied.

"What is your name?"

Daniel thought about it for a split second, realizing he had no identification on him.

"David Flannery," he responded. He knew there were Flannerys around here. None of them were named David. It was good enough. The Tans would have no idea.

"Why did you shoot my friend?" Daniel asked.

"Because I could."

The Brit was smirking.

"I may be mistaken, but I think there are laws against shooting people merely because you want to," Daniel said.

"There might have been before, but things are different now. It is open season on you soup-takers."

Daniel knew "soup-takers" was slang the British used to describe the Irish who converted to Protestantism during the potato famine. Many had done so to keep from starving. The Delaney clan had not been among them. The men left him again to get the horses loaded and to tend to their friend, who was barely clinging to life.

At the Delaney camp, several men were preparing to ride out and find John when Michael rode up. He had traveled all night. Nobody but Michael could have made such a journey in the dark. He got a fresh horse and joined the men in pursuit of his two brothers.

John was pushing hard now to find Daniel. It had only been light for a couple of hours when he spotted the smoke from the soldier's fire. They had not yet broken camp. Staying out of their sight, he circled until he found a high spot to work from. He tied his horse up and crept close enough to see what was going on. He carried two long guns and a pistol. He saw two men standing over his brother, who was tied to a tree. They were taking turns kicking Daniel.

John had a clear shot at one of the men. He squeezed off a shot that rang through the canyon like music in the clean, fresh air. The ball entered the man's side right below his rib cage. He stumbled a few steps before dropping to the ground. The other fellow hit the ground too, looking for cover. He had no idea where the shot had come from. He was unarmed. The man by the fire looked sick, but he mustered enough strength to crawl over to the guns. John pointed his long gun.

Both men were looking around. They had no idea where John was. The man on the ground appeared too weak to lift his gun. John kept watching them. There was no urgent need to fire. They had not located him yet. As John tried to assess his brother's condition from afar, he noticed the man on the ground start to raise the rifle and aim it. John took aim and buried a shot deep into his chest.

As the other man tried to get up, John rushed toward him, pointing his handgun as he ran. He had no intention of shooting. Daniel was too close.

John shouted to Daniel in Gaelic, asking if there were only three.

"Yes."

"Stay where you are," John ordered the soldier.

John was close enough now to know he could easily place a bullet in the man. The man knew it too, so he obeyed, lifting his hands in the air.

John untied his brother and secured the soldier. Daniel had a serious head wound. It was no longer bleeding but it didn't look good. His upper lip was swollen from being slapped around and it was trickling blood. However, his brother's lower left leg was John's primary concern. It was badly swollen. After checking the fallen soldiers, John doctored Daniel the best he could. He cleaned the head wound, cut the boot off, and gave Daniel the whiskey bottle to ease the pain.

Next, John went through the belongings of the soldier. He was getting everything loaded up when Michael and the others rode in. John hugged his big brother and whispered in his ear.

"His leg is bad. He needs to see a doctor."

Michael nodded, smiled at John, and knelt beside Daniel, who was drowsy from whiskey and lack of sleep, but happy to see Michael.

"What happened?"

As Daniel told him about it, John and the others were putting together a makeshift pallet for Daniel's transport home.

They were loaded and ready to travel when Michael came over to John.

"I am proud of you. You saw what needed to be done, and you acted quickly. I think you did well."

"Is Danny going to be all right?"

"Don't know yet. I am going to take him to Mother. They will have a doctor there. She will know what is best. Grady and I will handle this. I need you to hold your prisoner here until I get back. There is more information I can get from him. I'll return as soon as I can."

"What else do we need to do?"

"Nothing now. John, you must oversee your group alone now. Can you do it?"

John nodded.

"Good. Get word to Sean. I want everyone together when I get back. I need to talk with Father about a few things.

"I can take care of this," John assured him.

"John, I want you to know how proud I am of you."

"You already said so. You are starting to sound like Patrick, repeating yourself," John said, as the brothers hugged.

Meanwhile, as the Delaneys were reacting to Conway's altered strategy for Western Ireland, the man himself was again dealing with his troublesome son. As Conway was preparing to return, word had arrived from Galway that William was once again the center of an embarrassing episode. William was in jail waiting for his return. After his triumph in London, everything appeared to be going as planned. Now this. It was becoming obvious William could not remain in Ireland. He was too much of a liability. Conway did not have time for such distractions.

CHAPTER 5

Home

Molly had never been happier. Her husband was at home now and they were doing what she loved. Nelly was enrolled in school and was attending Mass with her. She still worried about the boys but was confident Mickey had trained them well and they would be safe. She was happy Patrick had found a girl he was interested in. She knew he was serious about her. Mickey was not as happy about his selection, but he had stopped commenting on the situation. It did no good and it only caused strife.

"When do I get to meet your Lucy?" Molly asked.

It was after dinner one evening as they sat around the table. Patrick looked at his father, concerned about this conversation in his presence. Mickey shrugged. It was his way of saying; "Go ahead."

"Would you like to go to town with me tomorrow? I need to pick up some things," Patrick asked his mother.

"Pick up things?" his father said under his breath. "You make a lot of trips to Galway and come back without much to show for it."

"Yes of course I would," Molly interrupted. "I need to buy some fabric. I plan to make Nelly and Elizabeth matching dresses. Would you like to go, Nelly?"

"May I?"

"Yes of course. You can help me pick out the material. I was thinking about some pretty pearl or ivory buttons down the front."

Mickey got up, shook his head, and walked off to find Finnegan.

They left early the next morning. It was a pleasant ride in the wagon, with Patrick singing to the ladies he loved. Patrick had a fine tenor voice and he loved music. When they arrived, he dropped the girls off at the store and arranged to meet them later at the hotel restaurant. Patrick hurried to the Conway house. It had been several days since he'd last seen Lucy. He was eager for her to meet his mother and sisters.

"Get ready! We have an appointment in a bit," Patrick said as she opened the door.

"Where are we going?" she asked.

"It's a surprise."

She smiled at him and hurried upstairs. She loved surprises, but mostly she loved being with Patrick. And it was always good to get away from William, who would be coming down soon.

Patrick was minding his own business in the parlor when William walked in with a glass half full of whiskey. He glared at Patrick as he would have at a stray dog who wandered in off the street. Patrick ignored him.

"What business do you have here?" William demanded. "And what exactly are your intentions toward my cousin?"

Patrick glanced at him. He looked out the window, continuing to ignore him. It was making William angry.

"I expect an answer when I address you," William continued, with an air of superiority. This came naturally to him.

Patrick slowly stood to face him. He looked him in the eye without saying a word and held his gaze. Patrick knew he was winning the day with his silence. William was fuming as he took a step forward. Patrick maintained eye contact and said nothing as he took two steps toward

William. They were only two feet apart.

Before anything could happen, Wallace Conway walked in on the two of them. He was sober enough to sense things were tense.

"William, can you please come with me? I need your assistance. I should appreciate your input on a critical matter I'm dealing with," he said.

Never had he needed young William's opinion on anything, and he probably would never ask again. It was all he could think of on the spur of the moment. Wallace was rather pleased with himself.

"I am busy right now," William said as he sipped his drink.

"Come now my boy, it is rather urgent," Wallace persisted.

"I will be seeing you again. I am not finished," William sneered at Patrick.

He turned and left the room with Wallace, who ushered him into a room he had commandeered for an office. He closed the door as Lucy came down the stairs in a beautiful pink dress. Her thick auburn hair was brushed perfectly with a matching pink bow set behind her right ear.

"Do I look all right?" she asked. "You know I have no idea where we are going."

"You look perfect.

Patrick was happy when he and Lucy arrived at the restaurant before his mother and sisters. He arranged for a table away from the kitchen entrance. He ordered a bottle of wine and appetizers as his mother and sisters arrived.

"Mother, I'd like for you to meet Miss Lucinda Conway."

He could not help but notice Lucy's face glowing as he introduced his family. It was the same sparkle he had seen in her eyes and the same lovely smile that had drawn him when they first met. It had not lost its appeal in the least. Lucy rose like a fine lady and offered her hand to Molly. Molly ignored her hand and gave her a hug and a gentle kiss on the cheek.

"I have heard so much about you, but Paddy failed to tell me how beautiful you were,"

Lucy and Patrick both blushed as Molly continued.

"Please call me Molly, and this lovely child is Nelda Louise, but we call her Nelly. And Nelly is holding our youngest, Elizabeth."

Nelly did her best to hug Lucinda with one free arm and the other arm full of squirming toddler.

"So, pleased to meet you both! Patrick did not tell me you were coming. I would have brought a token."

She looked lovingly at Patrick to let him know she would have preferred some preparation on his part.

"If you would excuse me, I need to find the lady's room to care for the baby. She hasn't eaten in a while and I know she needs to be changed. Nelly, you stay with your brother. I'll be back soon," Molly said.

"I am going to school now," Nelly began, eager to strike up a conversation with the beautiful lady.

"Wonderful. How old are you?"

"I am eleven."

Nelly looked at the food and then at Patrick.

"Please, please! Eat! The food is delicious here," Lucy said, passing her a tray of sandwiches.

Nelly ate as she chatted with Lucy like they were old friends. When Molly returned, they ordered their meal. The conversation flowed as they enjoyed the food and company. Patrick was pleased his mother approved of Lucy; he could tell Lucy was enamored with his family as well.

Molly and the girls were still in town with Patrick when Michael and Daniel arrived home. Michael had sent a man ahead to fetch the doctor so he would be waiting at the house. Daniel's leg was still swollen badly, and the bone needed to be set. The doctor was relieved infection had not set in, and he predicted the bone should heal properly, though Daniel would need to stay off it for several months.

After the doctor left and Daniel was resting in a real bed, Michael and his father wandered off to talk about what had happened. They both had information about what Conway was doing—Michael from the man they had captured and Mickey from informants he had all over the region. Conway was bringing in more troops and deploying snipers to shoot first and ask questions later. They had now experienced this tactic during the ambush, and they'd lost a good man.

Mickey had been thinking about this and he feared for the lives of his men. They needed a new strategy. He had one to share with Michael. Mickey told his son the British were playing the long game, using the law to defeat the Irish. This, combined with Conway's new aggressions, would soon be the end of them unless they adapted and used the Brit's game against them.

In 1850, the Reform Act had given every man in Ireland the right to vote. To qualify, one had to own property worth twelve pounds. Few Irish did. The only people with this kind of wealth were the English who had moved in. The permitted Irish voters amounted to only sixteen percent of the population. The Brits controlled the ballots.

Mickey had a plan to change the status quo. Over the past few years, he had appropriated significant funds from the English. He had been using this for munitions and other supplies. If he converted his strategy to increasing the wealth of Irishmen who would then vote the way he directed, they could increase the Irish vote to nearly fifty percent of the total. By employing people and paying them enough to qualify them as voters, he could enable the Irish to once again rule themselves. What could not be done by the sword could be accomplished at the ballot box. It was a new scheme but Mickey felt it could work if they kept it quiet. If the Crown found out what they were doing, they would simply amend the law, and all would be lost.

"We can't beat these people with guns," Mickey told his son.

"We can never give up our guns, they will kill us all. I am sure of it. We must kill more of them than they do us. It's our only hope," Michael said.

"Listen to me," said his father. "We are not going to give up the fight. We will continue to harass them, but our main strategy must be to be smarter than they are, not stronger. We must outsmart them. Beat them at their own game. They love to boast about how civilized they are. How their people rule the Empire. Well, we will now be those people if we can vote."

Mickey went on to tell him the details of his plan. The two of them were still planning when they saw the wagon coming with Patrick, Molly, and the girls.

"Not a word of this to your brother," Mickey said.

"What are you saying?" Michael asked.

"I am saying he is out of the business. He is courting a British girl. I do not want him to know anything about what we are doing."

"A British girl?"

"Yes, and it gets worse. Her name is Conway. And she is living in the same house as Thomas Conway."

"You cannot be serious."

"I'm afraid so. And the silence is for his good as well as ours. He must not know what we are doing, ever. He is still your brother and I want you to always be close. He is still a Delaney. But we must now keep him in the dark on anything we do."

When Molly found out about Danny, she abandoned everything and everybody else until she was sure he would be all right. Michael and the men left early the next day. They had plenty to do.

Mickey hired several more men to work on his farm, paying each of them enough money to push them into the voting category. He also set up several businesses in town, employing people to build schools and repair bridges. This would return Galway to its proper status as a prosperous town. These were all good things, but his actual purpose was to gather voters who would be loyal to him. He would control who was in office. They would be using the English's own money to bring them down. Michael's part would be to keep a low profile while continuing to protect the Irish and gain wealth by levying what Mickey referred to as an "invader's tax." By taking funds from the English, the Delaneys would use their enemy's money to purchase voters they would later use to defeat them.

Michael understood his role and had every intention of doing as his father had asked until two days later when he and his men ran across a group of thirty soldiers in a remote valley. They were setting up a staging area for raids on suspected rebels. Michael sent runners out to summon as many men as they had in the area. By nightfall, they had fifteen men. Michael laid out a strategy for dealing with this problem. After all the men understood his plan, they settled in to get a few hours of rest. John and Sean took Michael and walked away from the others.

"What are you doing? You know Paw said for us to keep a low profile. And attacking a company of soldiers with half the men they have is quite the opposite of a low profile," Sean said.

"We can do this. They don't know we are here. We will be in and out in no time. Buck up brother and show a little courage," Michael said.

"Courage has nothing to do with it. It is not only against what Paw said but also foolish. You know in these things anything can happen. Should we win, we will still lose a lot of men. Men we need. Men who have families."

Sean pressed his case fervently.

"What about you John?"

Michael had taken a step towards his youngest brother.

"Are you with me?"

"We are both with you," Sean answered for John. "But we both think it is foolish."

Michael paused, turned, and walked away a few steps. They both knew he was struggling to contain his anger. Michael had a hair trigger and this was likely to set him off. After a few silent moments, he turned to face them. He was stone-faced. His voice had a clear tone of authority.

"I have given you orders, and I expect you to follow them. I will not change them. The men will think I'm a coward."

"Or they will think you came to your senses," Sean said under his breath as he and John walked back to the camp.

An hour later John gently woke Sean and whispered in his ear.

"I'm going to do a little scouting I'll take a couple of men with me. If I'm not back when it is time to attack, tell Michael not to worry, I'll be there for the fight."

Before Sean could answer, John slipped out of the camp on foot, leading his horse and the two men he'd brought. John left the men halfway there and scouted the area on foot by himself. He was gone for almost three hours and they were beginning to think he had been spotted and was tied up in one of the tents. They were afraid to go back to Michael without him.

When John finally returned, he filled them in on what he had seen. He sent one man back to brief Michael. During the night, another group of soldiers had joined them, and now there were over fifty men. As they slept, he had gone from tent to tent, gathering up as many ammunition pouches as he could find. He dropped them all in a water barrel. This would render their long guns useless. They still had revolvers and their hand weapons, but the fight would be more equal now. He also found a couple of good vantage spots from which to do serious damage when the fighting began.

Michael was furious when Sean told him John was not back yet. He was on his horse looking over his men when the rider approached. It was a man named O'Neal.

"John said to tell you more men have arrived, and the number is probably up to fifty now."

Michael took in the information without changing his expression.

"He also said to tell you your plan worked, and he has wet down all the gunpowder pouches so their firepower will be restricted. He said to attack swiftly and furiously, as you've planned,"

"Ah. Anything else?" Michael asked.

"He found a couple of good spots to fire from, so when he hears your first shots, he and Billy will begin firing from both flanks. He said if you want to, it might be better to attack from the front and rear at the same time. I can show you a way to get down the creek."

"Sean. take four men and follow O'Neal. Move in as soon as you hear us. Come in fast and have your men yelling." Michael said.

"I like this plan you have," Sean said, with a wink and a smile.

"Shut up and get moving."

Michael and the seven men walked their horses in as close as possible. When he heard the soldiers' mares whinny, his men aimed at the tents and the few guards who were on patrol. Dawn was breaking when Sean and his men heard the first shots. The sun was at their backs as they rode hard, revolvers ready, yelling as they made it to the tents.

John was on the north side of the camp on his belly, aiming at the officer's tent. Billy was on the south side, behind a log. His rifle was steady as he aimed at whatever moved first. The soldiers hurried from their tents, most of them still in their underclothing, and began snatching up their long guns. The Irishmen were riding their horses around the tents and firing at whatever moved. John spotted a bugler ready to sound the alarm. It was a little late to wake the troops, but he knew different tunes signaled different formations on the battlefield, so to add to their confusion he aimed at the bugler. The shot was true and it entered the horn of his bugle, exploding metal in the man's face. He went down at the foot of the captain. John grabbed his second rifle and aimed at the captain's chest. The bullet entered his left shoulder and he spun around, back into the tent.

Michael was now off his horse, walking from tent to tent, killing everyone he met. Some soldiers fought with pistols and others ran. Billy was also doing a lot of damage from his position and he dropped quite a few soldiers. It wasn't long until all the shooting was over. The Irish had no fatalities, but three men were wounded. Six of the men were sent out to round up the stragglers. The rest were busy gathering the bodies of the slain soldiers.

Michael was looking over the battlefield when he saw John walking up his horse following him. Michael and his men were covered in blood, but most of it was English blood. John looked like he was ready for church.

"Glad you could join us. You look mighty fresh," Michael said.

"Only a little gunpowder I need to wash off," John said.

Michael walked over to him and hugged him. He whispered in John's ear.

"You did well boy. You keep making me proud of you."

"Well, I like to see a good plan come together. You are a great general."

John grinned.

Michael lovingly slapped the back of his head.

"You're a cheeky devil. I'll give you that," Michael said. "Let's get busy. It's going to be a long day cleaning this mess up."

They buried the dead, piling the tents and everything else flammable on top of the mass grave. As it burned, they looked for escaping soldiers. They found a few but some got away. Michael gathered his men together as the sun was going down. He swore them all to silence. Nobody was to talk about what had happened this day.

A few days later, Conway heard the news. He was furious.

While fortune had favored the Delaneys, young William was not as pleased with his current situation. He was in a Galway jail cell, nursing a headache caused by the combination of a severe hangover and a knot on his forehead he didn't remember getting. He was livid. After Lucinda left with the Irish gutter rat, he'd decided to visit Lady Priscilla's. It was not the best brothel in town, but it was the closest. The police were called because he had beaten a young girl. Before they arrived, several regular customers, encouraged by Lady Priscilla herself, had taken matters into their own hands. They'd beaten William severely. He was fortunate the police arrived when they did. He had no recollection of any of this, but it was all in the official police report. He would remain in jail until his father arrived, but not because he would be charged with a crime. He was being held for his own protection. The locals did not take well to their sporting ladies being abused.

"Get me out of here," William screamed again from his locked cell. "I demand you release me at once. Do you know who I am?"

"Yes, we know exactly who you are. Now shut up," said a big man from across the station.

It was not the answer William wanted. He was furious. And it was all Lucinda's fault. If she had shown him the respect he was due, he would not have had to go to the brothel. He vowed he would make her pay. She had no right to snub him and flaunt her affection for that dirty Irish scum.

While William was vengeful, Lucy was as happy as she had ever been. His not being around was exactly what she wanted. She had a wonderful time with Patrick's family. They were charming, warm, joyous people who loved each other. She longed for such a family. She loved her father, though he was a long way from charming, even when sober, which was rare. Learning William was being held in his own father's jail was particularly pleasing to her. She was tired of having to spend all her time avoiding him. His aggressive behavior toward her had grown increasingly alarming.

She wrote in her diary that she wanted to spend her life with the Delaneys. As she reviewed her entries over the previous few weeks, she realized she was consumed by two things: her joy over being with Patrick and her constant fear of William. She could not go on like this. The stress was more than she could handle.

CHAPTER 6

The War Escalates

Thomas Conway returned from London with one thing on his mind. He needed to meet with his captains to make sure they understood his plans. He was bringing in two groups of people with absolute authority. The first group comprised trained detectives, skilled at intelligence. Their task was to quietly determine who among the subjects were involved in the resistance. The second group also had a particular skill set. They were skilled marksmen—trained killers—experienced in India and other regions. Any Irishman they identified as a rebel would be executed in the field without a trial.

After he was certain his men understood and had been sufficiently threatened, he sent for his son. William was to be brought to the chief's office in chains. Thomas wanted to further humiliate the boy since William had humiliated the entire family for years. The prisoner was escorted by two burly policemen who left him to plead his case before his father, who looked on indifferently.

"Are you proud of yourself?" Thomas asked.

"Oh yes sir, my main objective is to make your life as miserable as you have made mine. So yes, I'd say yes, I am quite proud of myself. Now if you would please remove these chains, I can go on about my business of irritating you further," William said.

"Simpson," Thomas Conway called. "Take the prisoner back to jail. I have more pressing business."

Simpson did as he was ordered, and the same two officers marched William back to his cell. The Conway heir was so mad he was ready to kill someone. Anyone would do.

Up in the mountains, a day's ride from Galway, Michael reorganized his troops. He released most of the men with assurances they would be called up again if needed. He kept only the most experienced of his men. These were divided into five groups of five men each. Michael expanded their territories and gave them their orders. He chose three men to go from group to group, conveying information back and forth. All orders were to be verbal; he wanted nothing that might fall into the hands of the British. His forces must remain informed and nimble.

John had his group, consisting of himself and the four men he selected. They were a close group, most of them young. None were as young as John, but he was a Delaney. The Delaney name was enough to foster respect. Sean also had a group of men he knew and loved. For the next few months, the rebels would wage a different kind of war. Most of their activities were conducted at night and nothing was discussed with anyone not in the group.

Unbeknownst to Sean, one of his men was also working for the English. Roger O'Malley had been with Sean for years and was trusted, but the money he'd been offered by the English for being a double agent was more than he could refuse. The O'Malley family suffered like many Irish had through the entire potato famine. The money he received from the Brits was the only thing keeping his large family alive.

As the Delaneys fine-tuned their operation in the West, back in Galway, Conway again sent for his son. After another night in jail, William's manners had improved, and this time the conversation was civil. The young man had promised to behave himself and to look for a job, though he had no idea what he might do. Maybe he would try a few things to get the old man off his case. He was released to go home. Of course, there were no records of this arrest, nor would there be. William knew this. He knew the old man was stubborn and wanted to make a point. William was proud too, and he had a few points of his own to make.

After a few weeks, he was still unemployed. This was not because there were no jobs. There were plenty of people who wanted to hire the police chief's son. However, it soon became clear each job would require work William considered beneath his station. His dignity would not allow such an insult.

He had returned to spending most of his time drinking whiskey with Wallace. His father was not concerned as long as he caused no trouble. William had been minding his own business and staying away from the whorehouses, mostly because he was not welcome there after his last visit to Lady Priscilla's.

Wallace and his daughter had been invited to stay on after Thomas's return. Wallace was elated about it. Lucy on the other hand was not happy. She preferred the small flat in a dingy neighborhood over having to live near William. She and her father, who was rarely sober, could not agree, and she was without options.

The uneasy peace in the Conway house ended the day Lucinda came into her room and found William perched on her bed, reading her diary.

"You have no right to be in here, and you are violating my privacy. Give me my diary," Lucy demanded.

"It is you, little lady, who has no right. You come into our home and write vile things about the people who have shown you such kindness. Who do you think you are?"

"Give it to me!"

She marched over and attempted to take it from him. This was a mistake. William grabbed her arm. Holding her too tightly, he smiled, mocking her.

"Stop with all your demands you urchin. I have a few questions for you. What exactly do you mean when you say, *when I look into his eyes, it is like looking into heaven?*"

"And what about this," he said as he let her go to turn a few pages back.

"Here it is, *I see nothing but evil hatred when I look at William.* Are you a witch who can detect emotions at a glance?" he asked.

"None of this is your business," she said.

She was hurt and embarrassed.

He started laughing at her. It was not a pleasant laugh. He was scaring Lucy.

"Also, what do you mean by this?"

He flipped a few more pages and read.

"When I hear him refer to me as his girl, my entire body quivers."

"Give it to me and get out. Right now."

Her anger had turned to sheer panic and she was weeping as she spoke. He had no right to do this. She turned to leave the room. He was faster than she expected and he arrived at the door before her, shutting it and locking it. They were only inches apart. Too close for her comfort, she could smell the whisky on his breath and sense the primitive lust in his eyes. She started to back away from him and he grabbed both her arms. He was strong. He was hurting her.

"Let me go."

He let go of one arm so he could grab her breast. She screamed. His hand left her breast to cover her mouth.

"Hush you idiot. We don't want to bother anyone. We need a little privacy."

He dragged her away from the door. She was terrified. As he pushed her toward the bed, his hand came off her mouth. She screamed again, turning her head so he could not muffle the sound. This scream was louder and longer. When he could not gag her with his hand, he slapped her hard across the side of the head. He picked her up and threw her on the bed, unbuttoning his trousers with an unpleasant leer. She screamed again.

"Please, help me!"

"Just you and me Lucinda. Lie back and enjoy it. I will show you what it is like to quiver all over," he said.

She tried to get off the bed on the other side, but he caught her by the foot and dragged her back. His shirt was unbuttoned and only his underclothing covered him. She tried to scream again but nothing came out. He pulled her close to him. He was now concentrating on getting her clothes off. She screamed again. This time she was audible. He stuffed his shirt into her mouth.

There was a knock on the door.

It was Patel.

"Mademoiselle, is something wrong?"

No matter how hard she tried, no sound would come through.

"Go away. We are fine," William barked.

"Are you sure?" Patel asked, in his heavy Indian accent.

"Yes, go away you idiot," William said.

He was now sitting on top of her and had succeeded in exposing most of her flesh. As he busied himself removing his underclothes, she managed to free one hand and jerked the shirt out of her mouth.

"HELP ME! HELP ME!" she yelled.

She heard Patel trying to get through the thick oak door. The iron latch held fast. William gagged her again as Patel ran down the stairs.

"We need to hurry now," William said.

Despite his superior strength and size, she was somehow able to escape him and roll off the bed. She climbed under the bed but he followed her to the ground, grabbed her by the hair, and pulled her out. She freed herself again before he grabbed both her ankles and pulled her away from the bed. He lifted her off the ground and slapped her hard.

She saw her opportunity then. She took hold of his right leg and pulled herself towards him. He lost his balance and fell backward. They landed hard but she was on top. Her next move was unplanned but effective. She bit down as hard as she could on his little toe, then shook her head back and forth like a terrier shaking a rat. He screamed and pushed her away. The toe was still attached, but barely. Blood was everywhere.

He was furious now and he tried to mount her again. She was out of breath and had stopped shouting. She wept, knowing she was losing the battle. He was too powerful. Suddenly they heard Patel.

"Open this door immediately."

"I should go away if I were you. We need a little privacy here," William said.

A shot rang out, then another shot, and another. Patel forced the ruined lock. William tried to get to the door before it flew open, but his damaged toe slowed him down. He was bleeding profusely. Patel saw what was happening and he swung the pistol. It landed flush with William's forehead and dropped him to the ground. Patel saw William was out cold. He turned away from Lucy to spare her dignity.

"Please get dressed, Miss Lucinda," he said.

He stood over the naked William, watching him. The blow to the head had rendered him useless. His plan was foiled.

Patel and two other servants wrapped up his foot and carried the unconscious William to Thomas Conway's office. Patel told his master what had happened. He left out nothing. It was a while before William came to. When he did, he was still half-naked, right back in the same jail cell he had been before. With as bad a headache as he had ever had and a barely attached toe, he was in bad shape.

After Lucy's wounds were cared for by a kind lady's maid, she was calm enough to gather herself when Patel knocked on her door again. From the hall, he reported that their belongings were packed and that he had arranged for them to be moved back to their flat.

He left a tea tray outside her door and suggested she pour herself a cup. It would help her relax. He stayed outside. He knew she would not want to see anyone for a while.

After the interruption caused by his son's latest indiscretion, Thomas returned to the work at hand. He was reviewing the weekly reports from his captains. He was pleased that except for the massacre in the highlands which he was trying to keep quiet, each week there showed significant progress. He was once again feeling in control. Order would soon be restored. Proper British society would be ushered in. Despite what the Irish renegades thought, this was what Western Ireland needed.

Thomas put the reports aside and thought about his son. He would need to get involved with this. He knew Patel had done what he had to do, and he also realized his servant was thoroughly upset over the brutal attack on Lucinda. It was now more than a family matter, however. Thomas would need to wrap this up before it got out of hand.

He sent word to the jail that William was to remain in his cell, alone and naked, until further notice. When Thomas arrived home, he was told Wallace and his daughter had moved back to their previous address. He went to them immediately.

He projected as much kindness as he could muster as he sat down with Wallace and Lucinda.

"My dear, I understand it will be hard for you to talk about this," he said. "Naturally, you will not want to discuss this, however, it is my duty as an officer of the Crown to gather all the necessary information. Please tell me in your own words what happened today."

Lucinda shook her head. She could not say a word. Wallace shrugged. Thomas asked again, still in a kind manner, but with a more pressing intonation.

"Can we do this another time?" her father asked.

"No, we cannot. It will be done now," he said firmly. "Tell her she must talk to me now."

Wallace pleaded with his daughter to comply. Lucy noticed her father was sober for the first time in a long time. Seeing him sober took her back to the days before her mother had died. This memory of her mother temporarily eased her pain. She also knew Thomas would not quit until he got his way. Without looking at him she told him what happened. Her father went outside, he could not bear to hear it again.

The chief listened and took notes as she told him every detail of the horror his son had caused. The only thing she omitted was the contents of her diary. He would never know what she had written. Her diary was safe now in a hidden place, never to be seen by anyone again. Lucinda was wise enough to realize he was not gathering her story to ensure justice was done. He was primarily concerned with making sure his family name was not dishonored if word got out, and it always did. Gossip like this always traveled fast. Thomas wanted to manage this as well as he could. She also knew charges would never be filed. It was the social aspects that concerned Thomas. When he had heard everything, he walked outside to find Wallace.

When they were outside together Thomas handed Wallace an envelope. Wallace glanced inside the envelope and saw the cash. A lot of it. Thomas saw his eyes light up. This was the reaction he wanted to see.

"I offer this token to help you both get through this."

He put his hand lovingly on his cousin's shoulder.

"It would be the best thing for Lucinda if this were not mentioned again. I am only thinking of what is best for you both," said Thomas.

Wallace knew his silence was being bought. He looked at the money again, then nodded his head in agreement.

"Then we will leave it at that," he said, as he turned and walked away.

CHAPTER 7

Families at War

It did not take long for news of William's attack on Lucinda to reach the Delaneys. Molly decided it was best if Patrick did not know right away. Mickey agreed, thinking his son might do something they all would regret. Of all the Delaney boys, he was the least likely to fly off the handle, but he was still a Delaney. Mickey feared what he might do.

After visiting with Lucinda, who was still greatly traumatized, Molly realized she would need to stay to nurse the young girl through her recovery. Wallace rented a hotel room so the ladies could have the house to themselves. It had been years since he had dealt with anything other than making sure he had enough whiskey to numb his senses and forget his disgrace. The Conway hush funds kept him well supplied with whiskey as he continued to abdicate his parental duties. In the meantime, Lucy needed a mother and Molly was there.

The first night Molly didn't ask Lucy to talk—she simply held her close until the girl dropped off to sleep The next morning after breakfast it was different.

"I need you to tell me about it," Molly said.

"I could never tell you. I can never tell anyone. I'm so… ashamed," Lucy said as she looked away from Molly.

"We must get you through this. You must talk about it. You can't keep it bottled up."

"I'm soiled. You will never see me the same way as you did before, and neither will Patrick," Lucy whispered.

"Oh, my dear why would you think such a thing?" Molly asked.

"Because it must have been partly my fault, I never should have written my thoughts. Not about someone like him," Lucy said.

"Why, the Conways are no better than anyone else," Molly said.

"You are wrong. They are better. They are above the law. They do as they please and nothing will ever happen to them. They know it. They see themselves as better than us. But I still wrote those foolish words."

Lucy was trembling now. Fear had gripped her at the thought of William. She began shaking her head and mumbling to herself. Molly held Lucy. She began to sing softly in her ear. After Lucy was calm, Molly began again.

"Lucy, nobody can harm you now. We will not allow it, trust me," Molly said.

"Yes, they can. You don't know these people," she said.

"Ah, but I do know them—and their kind. And there was a time when I was afraid of them. But I learned to stand up against them. You too will learn this. I will see to it. You are strong. You can do this. But first, you must tell me all about what happened. You cannot keep it in," Molly said.

"You will hate me," Lucy said. "I'll never be the same. I'm ruined by this."

"No, you are not, and I could never fail to love you. You have done nothing wrong. He is an evil man. It is no fault of yours. Do you hear me? You are not to blame. It is William who was wrong, not you. It's he who deserves the blame. Take a deep breath and start at the beginning."

In the meantime, Mickey's new companies were prospering. Converting working people into voters was happening faster than planned, and most of the enterprises were making a profit. All the proceeds were being plowed back into the companies so more people could be hired.

Ryan Sullivan was a young man Mickey was grooming to run as the representative in their district. The Governor, who was appointed by the crown, worked with an Executive Council. This consisted of other appointed individuals both political and military. It also had ten elected representatives. Mickey figured if eight of the ten elected representatives were his people, they could begin making changes. He knew they would not be able to take control immediately, but eventually, they would be able to do some real good. It was the only shot they had.

This needed it to work because the people were growing tired of the violence. Too many innocent men were turning up missing. They all knew what was happening. Mickey would have enough voters by the next election to get Ryan in office. Dublin had a good man in place there, so he only needed six more representatives. This meant he needed to travel again. Molly supported this since the trips were intended to be free of violence.

Mickey had sent word to his boys to stop everything and send all the men home. He needed Michael and Sean to help as he started new businesses in six different parts of the state. The Delaneys were well known which would ensure the success of the ventures.

John was to return home to work with Finnegan, Patrick, and Daniel. Molly would be getting her family together with this plan. She was tired of worrying about which boy might get hurt next.

Ryan Sullivan would be elected in the Galway district. This should be easy. Michael would work in the highly populated Dublin area. This was the most challenging area and would take the most money. He took most of his people with him. Belfast was already in place. They needed to secure only a few more voters there. It was easy to do with so many men needing work.

Daniel would be sent to Donegal in the northwestern area when his leg was healed. Loyal men should be easy to find there. Many had already fought alongside the Delaneys. Mickey took care of County Mayo. It was slightly north of Galway, close enough to allow him plenty of time at home with the family. Only Cork was left, and Sean would ensure it had plenty of voters.

A few days after Molly left, Mickey and Finnegan were watching their sheep graze in a lush green pasture near the River Shannon. The two of them were arguing over the total number of sheep they had in this field. It was their usual banter. Mickey estimated low because he was a natural pessimist, while Finnegan had a more realistic nature. He called it as he saw it. If Patrick had been there, his estimate would have been much higher, as he was the optimist. As they were each making their case, they saw Patrick riding up. He was in a hurry. They both knew what this meant. He had found out about Lucy.

"Where is Mother?" Patrick asked, as he jumped off his horse and walked towards them.

"She went to Galway," Finnegan said.

He wanted to be the buffer between the two of them. This conversation might not go well.

"Why did she go to Galway?" asked Patrick.

"Why did you go all those times? You never told us what you were doing. I suppose the two of you are more alike than we thought," Finnegan said

"When were you going to tell me about Lucy?" Patrick demanded.

"Who told you about it?" his father asked.

"Does it matter?"

"As long as your mother doesn't think I told you, I don't care how you found out," Mickey said.

Without another word, Patrick turned and went toward his horse.

"Hold on a minute," Mickey said.

Patrick turned to glare at them both.

"The boy you are going to see is no longer there," said Mickey.

"How do you know?"

"Have you forgotten who you are talking with? I'm not riding with your brothers but that doesn't mean I don't have resources."

"Where is he?"

"He will soon be on a ship bound for London. One of the O'Connell boys is watching him. We will know exactly where he ends up. And at the appropriate time, we can deal with him. He will not get away with this. Trust me, son. Now, you need to go see your lady friend. My guess is she would rather have you with her than out there chasing young Conway. Women are like that."

"And bring Molly back with you," Finnegan said. "I'm getting tired of your father's cooking."

Patrick knew his father was right. He would get to Lucy as quickly as he could.

William was waiting on board the ship to London after being escorted by several burly officers with orders to ensure the ship did not leave without him. He was glad to be leaving this hellhole of a country. He did not like the way he had been treated. His rotten bastard of a father had not said a word to him. His anger was growing by the minute as he stewed over his situation. As mad as he was at his father, it was nothing compared to the hatred, he had in his heart for the Irish dog who had ruined his life.

William convinced himself it was all Patrick's fault that he had been deprived of what he wanted. Without the Irishman around, Lucinda would have certainly been interested in him. She had been lured away. If he had been able to make her his, nobody else would have wanted her. He had been so close. The more he thought about it, the more bitter he became.

Danny O'Connell had booked passage on the same ship. He sat on a cargo box, playing his harmonica and watching Conway. It was an easy job. The young fool was so self-absorbed he had no idea what was going on around him. Danny's only hope was when it came time to take care of this English pig, it would be his knife to slit his throat.

Several months later, after Thomas had shipped his son back to his mother, where he belonged, all was quiet. Reports from his wife, who was not pleased to be responsible for their problem child, noted that William was keeping to himself. She had no idea what he was doing. He left their house around noon each day and she didn't see him until the next day. According to the house servants, he usually arrived home at ungodly hours. As long as he was staying away from her friends, it didn't matter what he did. Of course, the police knew what he was doing. Thomas Conway had his people in London ensure young William didn't further embarrass the chief.

On the business front, Peel had signaled he was pleased with the progress being reported to him. Except for the unusually harsh winter they had gone through, it looked like Thomas Conway's business, and his personal life had calmed down considerably.

Thomas had now hired his cousin Wallace to work for the Police Department, keeping their books. Though he did not want the alcoholic around, he needed to keep him close to ensure the man's compliance. The entire sordid affair with Lucinda and William was now considered a misunderstanding. The official record did not allow the authorities to determine guilt since their stories varied. William's official statement was she had lured him into her room. What he had actually said was that she deserved what she got. He only wished he had finished what he set out to do. While most people knew what had happened, they also expected the outcome to be exactly what it was. This class of society was above the law by which ordinary people were required to abide.

Patrick was now visiting Lucy daily. She would never completely recover from the incident. She had frequent dreams of being attacked by a beast trying to kill her. The beast looked like a wild hog, but it spoke with a man's voice. It was trying to eat her alive. It helped to have Patrick around. She felt safe with him and he was determined to stay near her to ensure nothing harmed her ever again. Danny O'Connell reported from London that William was keeping a low profile. Danny paid a local street urchin a few shillings a week to keep tabs on him, then he returned to Galway.

Daniel's leg had healed and he was back to working with John on the farm. There was nothing Daniel liked better than keeping things stirred up. It was all done in fun and the entire family expected this from him. It was hard not to like Danny. He was everyone's favorite, and he knew it. His personality drew people to him. He would be leaving soon so they all enjoyed him while they could. Little Elizabeth was walking now and it was hard to keep up with her. Like Nelly, she had an unquenchable curiosity

Back in Galway, the chief detective assigned to work with Conway was Orson Peterson. They were working late one evening, going over the information his men had collected. Peterson was more than a detective. He was considered the finest expert on criminal justice in the empire. He had an extensive background in law enforcement, and he was also a professor of Social Science at Oxford. He had written a book regarded as the bible in police circles and he was a man to be taken seriously. There was a reason Peel sent him to work with Conway. As Thomas Conway was getting up to leave, Peterson cleared his throat.

"Let's take a closer look at what we have here," he said as if talking to his students.

"What do you mean? I have seen all the reports," Conway said.

He could read and he was not pleased with Peterson's condescending tone.

"Most of the recent information points in one direction. We have had a significant change in the behavior of the resistance. They are no longer grouping in bands to conduct raids. They have dispersed and their illegal activities have almost completely stopped."

"And this is good news," said Conway. "Which means only one thing. What we are doing has been successful. If we redouble our efforts, we can eradicate them for good. We have broken their backs and now we should finish them off."

He was pleased his plan had worked. He started to get up again. Peterson sat there smoking his pipe. He motioned for Conway to sit back down as if to a disobedient student. Anger was bubbling up in Conway. He was ready to tell him the man off when Peterson continued`.

"Perhaps it's one way to handle it, but your method has the most risk. Let me explain."

Conway sat back down, more perturbed than before.

"Eliminating people has two main effects. One is good and the other is bad. We must weigh the cost. The good thing is the criminals will no longer be involved in their nefarious acts. The bad thing is the effect their elimination has on society."

"You are speaking in riddles. I am not one of your students. Get to the point," Conway said.

"For each one we eliminate, we stand the risk of creating seven others. Statistics show every man has between five and eleven people who care enough about him to take definitive action. In other words, we have given the rebels a cause — a recruiting tool more effective than any conscription the empire possesses.

"If we use seven as the integer midpoint, we can conclude that for each man we kill, at least seven will replace him. The number is multiplied if the killing is compressed over a short period. People must be given time to forget their losses. In other words, we can kill a few hundred and see them replaced by several thousand."

"Go on," Conway said.

Peterson had stopped talking—for effect and to light his pipe.

"The other method to handle this is as effective, but without the risk. Frankly, the empire is not in a position now to begin pouring more soldiers into a place which produces little other than a steady stream of workers for the poor house."

"Would you like a drink?" Conway said, pouring two glasses of brandy.

"Yes, a drink would be good. And now, I am going to make this clear to you. I will also tell you how clear this is to the Crown, which has every interest in ensuring success. First, we must realize the Irish are more sophisticated than the normal pagans we deal with. The proof is in how quickly they altered their behavior once they detected a superior force. When their violence stopped working, they adopted a new strategy before we realized what they were doing."

He paused again to repack tobacco into his pipe.

"But now we know what they are doing. A man named Michael Delaney has devised a plan they are now implementing. Sufficiently enriched with funds he has stolen from the Crown, he has now made it his mission to create Irish voters. This is being accomplished strategically so he can personally determine the outcome of our elections. For now, it is completely legal. To counter this attempt at subverting justice we shall act legally and swiftly to put Mr. Delaney out of politics for good."

They stayed in Conway's office until dawn, drinking brandy and defining the role Conway must play.

CHAPTER 8

A New Kind of War

By spring Mickey, had everything going his way. The boys came home when they could, staying busy creating voters. Potential voters were easy to find since most people needed work. Word had gotten around about the opportunities the Delaneys were creating. The main task was screening rather than recruiting. Patrick and Lucy were engaged to be married in the fall. She was going against her family and there would be consequences, but she did not care. She wanted nothing to do with any of them. She wanted to be a Delaney.

Though what she had been through with William would be with her always, she was doing her best to move on. Her love for Patrick and their approaching wedding gave her a spark of hope, but she knew she needed to avoid all contact with the Conways going forward. It worried her that her father was still working for Thomas. She was convinced the older man's heart was as dark as his son's. He was simply more devious.

William was becoming restless in London. He wanted to see the world. His father would not provide the necessary funds and William was not about to work for money like a commoner. He needed to figure out a way to get his father to pony up the money. The old man had plenty and as far as William was concerned, the stingy old coot was merely being stubborn. In retaliation, William was planning a trip back to Galway. He would move in with his father, and after a few weeks, he knew he could get the old man to pay whatever it took to fund his American expedition. He was enchanted with the adventure stories he had heard about the western frontier, and he thought he needed a fresh start.

Maggie Cartwright was still in bed, watching Thomas get dressed. She was a pretty nineteen-year-old. Because of Conway's position, he could not visit brothels like other men, so he had arrangements with a few establishments in town. He let them operate without the usual police intervention and they in return kept him supplied with young, attractive bedmates whenever he felt the need.

Maggie was a regular at the Conway estate because Thomas was fond of her. She was intelligent as well as pretty and well-mannered. All the girls were good at what they did, but her personality added something Conway enjoyed. He found the time he spent with Maggie was satisfying on multiple levels and he particularly enjoyed talking with her. He always wanted the other whores to leave as soon as their business was concluded but he liked to linger with Maggie. He found her not only charming but intellectually stimulating. Maggie also enjoyed her time in the Conway household, particularly after Thomas gave her access to his library and allowed her to entertain herself there in his absence.

"What are your plans today?" she asked as she sat up in bed, exposing the firm breasts Thomas so enjoyed.

"I have a meeting this morning at the station. Tomorrow, I need to be in Dublin so I will probably be leaving this afternoon. I should be back at the house by two. Why don't you make yourself comfortable here today? When I get back, we can have another go at it before I leave. I'll have Patel bring you up some breakfast."

"I'd be most grateful, sir. I started a novel last Wednesday when I was here, I can't wait to see how it turns out."

"Good. See you when I return."

He patted her on the cheek as he left the room.

After Conway left and she had enjoyed a nice breakfast, Maggie cleaned up and went downstairs. She was reading, but not a novel. She was busy looking through all the documents she could find. Thomas had an office in the library he used when he was at home. Over the past few months, she had discovered a lot of useful information. Maggie was an industrious young lady who made money not only by sleeping with wealthy businessmen but also by feeding information to Mickey Delaney. Most of the information she gave him he already knew, but he paid her anyway. It verified what he knew from his many other sources. She thought Mickey would be thrilled with what she had recently found. It was a list of all the informants who were feeding information to the police.

When Conway returned home, she was back upstairs with the novel. She chatted with him about various current events while he undressed, poured himself a stiff drink, and readied himself for more lovemaking. It had only been a few hours and he was proud of his prowess. His self-image was not in question when it came to the ladies.

He was finished with her after only a few minutes. As he dressed, she continued to praise his fine taste in literature, hinting she would like to stay at his house while he was away. He liked the idea of having a young girl ready for him when he returned. Thus far she had been careful and discreet about their relationship. He agreed she could stay but warned her to remain out of sight.

When he was gone, she went back to the library to continue copying the list. She was finishing the work and putting things back as they had been when she heard a carriage stop outside. She peeked out the window and saw William ordering the servants to gather his baggage.

She hurried upstairs to hide in Thomas's bedroom. The last thing she needed was for Conway's son to find her there. She decided it was time to make her move. She packed up the few things she had and waited until she thought it was safe to leave. She could not afford to be stopped because she had the list with her. If it were found, she knew she would be put to death. She eased through the door and tiptoed toward the back stairs used only by the servants. She gasped when she saw William seated on the top step, waiting for her.

"Well, who do we have here?"

"I am leaving," she said, still startled.

"I see. The question I have, however, is what business does a woman like you have sneaking around this house?"

"I wasn't sneaking! I have permission to be here,"

She stepped past him and bounded down the stairs as fast as she could. As soon as she was out the door, she started running and she didn't stop for several blocks.

William laughed out loud. This was perfect. He came home to barter with his father for funds. Now he had better leverage than he could have hoped for. Rather than begging for his mercy, he could now blackmail the old pervert. Imagine the scandal when word got back to his mother that her husband had been entertaining a nineteen-year-old prostitute in the marital bed. This was too good to be true.

He went to the parlor, poured a glass of whiskey, and began to plot his next move. His luck was running high so he decided he would settle the other score he had. He was going to go see Lucinda and demand an apology. By now she was probably through with the Irish mutt and would be ready to show William appropriate respect. He was willing to overlook her ruining his toe. It was her choice. She could make it easy on herself or rough. Either way, he was not going to be humiliated again. He would get what he wanted — what he deserved.

When Conway returned, he went directly to his office. His manservant Patel was waiting for him.

"Master William is back," Patel said.

It was all he needed to ruin his day. Thomas had returned from a productive trip. He had received lavish praise from everyone for the remarkable progress against the rebels. Never mind that it was not his idea. He had no problem taking credit for the ingenious solution that would bring civility to the entire Island. He was looking forward to returning home to Maggie. Instead, he faced an unpleasant confrontation with William.

William was not at home when Thomas arrived, but was swapping adventure stories with the locals at a notorious bar. He would soon be famous so they should remember they once drank whiskey with him. They had no problem acting as if they believed all his tales since he was the one buying the drinks. Nodding in agreement was a small price to pay for a glass of good whiskey.

Danny O'Connell was one of the locals enjoying the free whiskey. He was assigned to keep up with William, so as soon as he learned young Conway was back in Galway, he got to work. His job was only to watch him unless he endangered Lucinda. If Lucinda was threatened in any way, Danny could act. Danny took this as good news. He figured it would be only a matter of time before he would be cutting the boy's throat.

It was late when William returned home and Thomas was waiting for him.

"Who told you you were welcome here?"

"Good to see you, too," his son replied with a smile.

Drunk or not ,Thomas was going to deal with this tonight.

"I'll slap the smile off your face," he said, as he moved across the room toward his son.

"I'll bet you don't," William said, "and let me tell you why. You see I am under an unusual amount of stress. Imagine the emotional trauma I felt as I came home to find my mother's bed was being occupied by a street whore. The police chief, a respected pillar of the community, has been keeping a sporting woman in his bed—in the very bed he has vowed to share only with his loving wife."

William walked over and poured himself and his father a drink.

"I came here with a proposition I'm sure you will be interested in hearing."

He went on to explain his wild scheme with the estimated cost. Thomas listened quietly. When William finished, he told his father he would be expecting an answer in the morning.

"Sleep on it," he said, "since you will be sleeping alone tonight."

When Wallace found out William was in Galway, he became worried about his daughter. Before he went to work the next day, he went through his belongings and came out with a pistol. He checked to make sure it was functional, then loaded it and handed it to Lucinda.

"Why are you giving me this?" she asked.

"No reason. I simply want to make sure you have it in case you need it," Wallace said, without looking at her.

She knew it was a lie.

"He is back, isn't he?" she asked.

Wallace ignored her, acting as if he did not hear her.

"Father, when did he get back?"

"Yesterday."

He turned and went to the office. She was strangely moved that her father cared enough to think of protecting her. It had been years since he thought about anything except where his next drink was coming from.

Lucy spent the day making sure she was only a few steps away from the revolver. She knew how to use it and she would if she had to. Several times she thought she saw William walking across the street. Maybe it was her imagination. She was not sure.

Later there was a knock on the door. She grabbed the gun and inquired who might be there. She was relieved when she heard Patrick's voice. She opened the door, still holding the pistol at her side. He looked at the terror in her eyes and the weapon in her trembling hand.

"He's back, Patrick."

She dropped the pistol and threw herself into his arms, sobbing.

C H A P T E R 9

Stalking

Several days later, Danny O'Connell was watching as William walked back and forth across the street from the house. It was obvious the young Conway had evil intentions. This was the second day Danny had spent watching the house, still under orders from Mickey. Earlier, Lucy had left to go to the market. She didn't feel safe, though, even with the revolver Wallace had given her in her handbag.

She was returning from the market with her hands full of parcels when she heard his voice.

"Good to see you, Lucinda."

She did not know if she could get to the gun in time.

"Leave me alone."

She crossed the street to avoid him.

"I only want to speak with you," William said.

"I have nothing more to say to you."

She had not turned to look at him, but she knew he was close.

"We need to clear up this mess—this misunderstanding. You know you led me on. You led me to believe you were interested in me."

"Leave me at once," she said.

Her voice was trembling as fear gripped her. He could hear it in her voice and it brought a smile to his face.

"You invited me to your room. Admit it. You only got upset because I read your silly diary. You accused me of vile things. But if you apologize, I am ready to forgive you."

"Stop following me. Go away."

She could barely get the words out. He knew how afraid she was. He had control of her. She was his now.

"Think about what I've said. If we put this behind us, things could be good for you. I could make life very nice—or not."

He said the *'or not'* in a threatening tone. It sent chills down her spine. With his last terrifying words hanging in the air, he left her. She turned to see him limping away. His toe had not healed properly.

Danny was ready to pounce on William if he laid a hand on her. He followed the boy to a local tavern, then went to find Patrick. Danny was doing as expected, gathering information on William. After he reported what had happened, he assured Patrick that if William dared touch Lucinda, he would cut him to pieces and feed him to the hogs.

Later that evening. Patrick returned to the house. Wallace was there but Lucy had already retired.

"He followed her today," Patrick said.

Wallace hung his head. What could he do?

"Tell me about William," Patrick said.

"What do you want to know?"

"I want to know everything there is to know. Tell me everything you know or have ever heard about him. This is important."

Wallace Conway spent the next few hours telling Patrick all he knew about young Conway. He did it without a drink in his hand, which was hard for the old alcoholic.

Meanwhile, In a small cottage not far from Sunrise Estates, Maggie sat around a table with Mickey Delaney and several other men. They were going over the list Maggie had copied for them. Maggie would never return to the Conway house. She had been saving her money and had enough now with what she had earned from this transaction to move away and start a new life—somewhere far away, where nobody knew what she had done for a living in Galway. Mickey had arranged for her to go to Dublin and work for one of his businesses. She hugged him and left with one of the men. The others remained to discuss exactly how they would deal with the traitors.

When Molly learned about William's visit, she dropped everything she was doing and hurried to Galway. She packed Lucinda's belongings and moved her immediately to the Delaney estate, out of William's reach. Lucy was more than happy to leave. Wallace was also happy to see her out of harm's way. He could not protect her. She was safer if she was nowhere near the Conways.

Molly moved Patrick into the cottage behind the main house where Finnegan was living. Finnegan was weaker by the day. Molly was afraid he had cancer. Some believed cancer might be contagious, so she wanted him away from the girls, but close enough that she could care for him. He had always been a slender man, but now no matter what he ate, he was little more than skin and bones. Patrick was glad to stay and care for his old friend.

It was not proper for Patrick and Lucinda to live in the same house before they were married. Presenting a proper front was important to Molly in case a priest came by. Mickey was worried about having a Conway in his house but he kept it to himself. He knew Molly well enough not to cross her on this.

Others were not happy about the move. William was furious when he discovered Lucinda had slipped out of his reach. Danny O'Connell was also unhappy. He had been looking forward to killing William sooner rather than later. William could not control himself. Danny knew these spoiled elites felt entitled to anything they wanted. And William had made clear what he wanted.

"Did you know Lucinda has been taken away to live with those

Irish peasants?" William asked his father.

"Yes, I am the police chief. Do you think I don't have sources? Do you think I don't know what is going on in my region?"

It made little difference to Thomas where she lived. He was more concerned with where Maggie was. He had been trying to find her for weeks. She had simply disappeared. He blamed his son for this.

"What are you doing about it?"

William pressed his father on the matter.

"Why should I do anything? Why do you care?"

It had now occurred to Thomas that his son might be smitten with Lucinda.

"Never mind why I care,"

William was not pleased with the direction of this conversation. They rarely talked and when they did, it was never pleasant.

"What difference should it make you? You will be leaving for America soon."

"Because it is the right thing for you to do, Father."

William had no better argument so he thought he might shame the old man into doing something. He knew pride was the main motivation for most of what his father did.

"I think you should at least know what is going on. Our family is being disgraced, you know. You should care about the family name if nothing else."

This resonated.

"As hard as it is for me to say this, you might be right."

Good, Thomas knew now he wanted her. He wanted her badly. This was better than he'd hoped.

He had regained the leverage he needed to rein in his son, as well as a good reason to visit the Delaneys.

"Let me think about it," Thomas said.

He sipped his wine and continued enjoying his perfectly prepared roast leg of lamb. William left the table to go wherever it was he went at night. Meanwhile, Thomas pondered the latest development.

For a long time, he had wanted to know more about the Delaneys. He wanted to see for himself. They had always been troublemakers. Now they were wealthy troublemakers. He didn't understand how they had become so affluent. The worst thing about their wealth was they were not merely buying possessions, like normal people. They were creating companies and making other rebels wealthy. And they were becoming popular. This was a problem.

He had contemplated sending an assassin to pick off Mickey Delaney. Though it would have been an efficient strategy, he knew this would not work. Mickey had become a local hero. Killing him would cause more trouble in the long run than he could gain from his absence. Then he smiled as he thought about the new advantage he'd uncovered. His useless son had suddenly become worth something, even if accidentally.

Mickey was in Cork on business when Thomas Conway and a group of detectives disguised as regular policemen showed up at the house. When they were spotted nearing the Delaney estate, Molly and the girls were escorted by two of their men to Finnegan's cottage. Patrick, Daniel, John, and six other men met the soldiers as they crossed the stream near the house.

"May I help you?" Patrick asked.

Everyone was armed so things were tense. Conway motioned to a policeman near him, who dismounted and walked over to Patrick with a piece of paper. Patrick took the paper from the man without taking his eyes off the police chief. Patrick handed the note to the man next to him. The man read it aloud. Then in Gaelic, he summed it up, wading through all the legal terms as best he could. The paper said that the police were going to search the entire property.

"Perhaps there is a place we can talk while my men do their work,"

Conway said, in a neighborly tone.

"You are welcome to come inside," Patrick said.

He nodded respectfully to the police chief. He turned his horse and galloped back toward the house. He told the men in Gaelic to let them see whatever they wanted.

"They are here to provoke us. Be polite and let me know what happens. If there is trouble, then I'll sound the alert. Do nothing until it is time."

"You must be Patrick Delaney," Conway said as he entered their home.

"I am. May I get you anything?"

"Yes, that would be nice."

"Follow me."

Patrick led Conway and his two men with him into the dining room. The other six men were busy searching the premises. Each man had an Irish escort watching every move. Patrick brought out bread, cheese, and cold mutton. He served it with mugs of recently-brewed dark beer.

"I was hoping to meet Mickey Delaney. I have heard much about him," said the police chief.

"He is away on business."

"Seems he has been very busy of late," Conway said.

He was fishing for a conversation about the enterprises the Delaneys ran. Patrick said nothing.

"What sort of business is your father in?"

"I am sure you already know. They are all legitimately registered businesses. I am sure you have had your men look into them."

The two of them talked for a while without Patrick saying anything of substance. He answered all the questions but said nothing. When Conway tired of this, he asked for Lucinda. He informed Patrick that he would speak with her alone. Patrick let him know he would be in the next room if needed.

Lucinda was uneasy as she studied the face of the man she judged to be equally as evil as his son. Conway tried to persuade her to come back to Galway. It was all a big misunderstanding. He knew she would never come back. He didn't care if she did. She was serving the purpose he wanted as his detectives were no doubt finding useful information.

After several hours, the detectives were wrapping it up. They were unable to discover anything useful. No matter how hard they tried, they could not provoke a confrontation. The discipline Mickey had taught his sons and the others was impressive. As they were leaving the barn, one of Conway's men made a last attempt. He backed into John, who was watching him. The policeman pretended to interpret the accidental touching as an assault.

The big man whirled around, swinging with all his might. The idea was to have a quick confrontation that would result in the arrest of a much-desired prisoner to escort back to Galway. They did not want to return empty-handed. His blow was aimed at the young Irishman's head. He was an enormous man so one punch would be enough.

The blow connected with nothing but air, however, as John ducked under the swing and backed away. John was a safe distance from the big man as he lost his balance and stumbled forward. The policeman regained his balance and rushed at John, who dropped to the ground, covering his head with both arms. As soon as John was knotted up on the ground, the full force of the charging policeman hit him hard. A heavy boot landed on his shoulder causing pain and numbness. But that pain was nothing compared to what the officer felt as he tumbled head over heels into the gravel covering the floor of the barn. Two things happened next. John popped up and moved clear of his adversary at the same time the man's fellow officer broke into a belly laugh. The man looked up to see John walking calmly towards the house. The policeman was bleeding from dozens of cuts and scrapes from the crushed gravel. He was cursing

John walked into the dining room to find Patrick and Conway sitting in uncomfortable silence. John told them both what happened. Patrick had now had all he could take. First Lucy, and now his little brother, Before Patrick could sound the alarm for his men to kill every soldier on the place, Conway saw the anger in the Irishman and he rose from his chair.

"Please accept my apologies. We will be leaving now."

With that, he and his men left. The men considered it a defeat. Conway, however, was pleased he had gotten what he wanted. The feud between the Delaneys and the Conways was official now. Scores would soon be settled in his favor, he was sure.

CHAPTER 10

The Plan

Mickey Delaney was returning from Cork when word reached him that Conway had paid them a visit. He'd known it would happen sooner or later. He was hoping for later. The election was getting close and he did not want any distractions.

He had now completed his dealing with the traitors discovered through Maggie's notes—all except Sean's friend, Roger O'Malley. The boys had grown up together and were close. He did not know what to do with the boy. He knew what to do with the others though. Each case was handled separately. Some of them had to be killed. Others were punished in various ways and were exiled from the cause. And some were forgiven. There was no rule book on how to run a rebellion. Most rebellions didn't last as long as this one had.

Mickey had spent his life fighting the British. In most ways, his instincts had served him well. His final decision about Roger was to defer. He would leave it up to Sean to make the decision. For now, he needed to see what Conway was up to.

Orson Peterson was once again sitting in Conway's office with his feet up on the desk, smoking his pipe. This time rather than being reluctant to meet with him, Thomas had invited the professor. He now knew the Delaneys were not like most Irish peasants.

"I can understand your concern and I share the same belief that this issue must be handled," Peterson said, as he looked over the reports he had requested.

"I need this to go well. This is the last obstacle," Conway said.

"I doubt it is your last. These things are never as easy as they appear. I do agree that it is a pressing concern."

"I'd like to hear what you think," Thomas said.

He was becoming impatient with the professor's ways of skirting issues. Thomas felt he only did it to show off.

"First, this should have already been taken care of," Peterson said.

"What are you saying?"

"I'm saying you waited until Delaney became a hero. Now killing him is out of the question. I agree the best way to kill a snake is to cut off its head. However, as I said, it is too late for that. What needs to be done now is to render him helpless. If we can take away his wealth, his ability to gain influence is gone. We need to make him a pauper."

"How do we do this?"

Finally, he was getting to the point and Conway appreciated it.

"I have a few ideas," Peterson continued after one of his long pauses. Conway took notes as Peterson laid out a detailed strategy.

The recent leverage William had gained with his father had changed the dynamics of their relationship completely. Thomas mostly ignored him, which was fine with his son. He did not know that his father had detectives watching him. Thomas knew it was only a matter of time before his son once again brought shame down on their family.

Because life was better now for William, he had decided to postpone his adventure to America. As soon as Thomas had time, he would need to take care of this problem. But for now, all his attention was on the Delaneys.

It wasn't long before detectives reported to Thomas on William's most recent antics. It was gambling this time. William had been caught using loaded dice at a local establishment. However, before it was detected that he was a cheat, he had taken all the money from a local ruffian named Jacob Sullivan. Because of this, William was now spending most of his time at home. Sullivan was no genius, but he knew better than to go to the police chief's house.

It was late summer when the arrangements were made final for Patrick and Lucinda's wedding. The ceremony was to be held at an Anglican Church, which did not please Molly. Nobody else in the family cared. All the family and friends would attend. The wedding was scheduled for a Sunday afternoon. It followed several days of partying and celebration. Though Wallace was the only family Lucinda had, he, too, was enjoying himself, mainly because alcohol was plentiful.

As the family began the procession to the church, William Conway rode up with several uniformed policemen. He didn't say a word as he got down from his horse and marched into the church to find the vicar. The policeman followed him and the Delaney men followed them.

Young William handed a note to the Vicar, then turned and addressed the crowd that had gathered.

"There will be no wedding today. Lucinda is carrying my child and she will return with me to Galway. We are to be married at once so that I may raise my child properly."

"You are a liar," Patrick announced. "She has never been with you."

"I am sure you are unaware of our love for each other," William said. "She was just having sport with you, pretending to care. It was all a game. When she and I got together we laughed at you. What a fool you have been to think that a fine girl with her bloodline would ever care for you."

Patrick had to be held back from attacking William as the local Vicar read the letter. The Delaneys were ready to put an end to William for good. The policemen with William sensed the danger and quickly rushed him away. But he had accomplished what he set out to do.

The wedding was postponed. Since William's claim had been made, it was determined that Lucinda would not be allowed to marry Patrick for another three months. If she were not showing signs of a baby by then, they could be married. Not one person there believed William, but to appease the priest they agreed to wait. The Delaney-Conway feud had reached a new high.

The next day Sean decided he had to deal with his problem.

"When were you going to tell me that you had another job?" he asked Roger O'Malley.

"I have no other job," Roger replied.

"You must have another job. Where else would all the money that you have been giving your family come from?"

"I'll tell you when I decide it's your business to know everything about me. Have you high and mighty Delaneys been nosing into my business?"

Roger was angry.

"Are you going to tell me or not?" Sean asked.

"I'll tell you when it is your business. Otherwise, I'll thank you to leave me and my family alone."

"Well, it turns out it is our business. We know it is money you received from the Brits for giving them information about us," Sean said.

He was trying to keep his emotions under control. He was getting angry that his closest friend was now trying to deceive him.

"Who told you that lie?"

"Nobody told us. We read it for ourselves from a document lifted directly from the police in Galway. I can tell you how much money and what information you gave the Tans to get it. Are you still going to pretend that you have no idea what I'm talking about?" Sean said.

"Yes, I am," Roger said, "And I want nothing to do with you Delaneys, ever again."

He turned and walked away. The conversation had not gone the way Sean had hoped it would. He was expecting a quick confession, a promise of loyalty, and a return to what they once had. He knew now that was impossible.

Molly took Lucinda to the doctor. She wanted her examined not because she believed William, but because she wanted everyone in the region to know what a scoundrel he was. Molly wanted Lucinda's reputation to be untarnished. The doctor ensured them that she was not pregnant and had never been with a man. The wedding was rescheduled for the following week. This time William Conway would not stop it.

The elections were a success. Every person the Delaneys had backed was elected. This was a major accomplishment for the Irish people. They now could have more of a say in their lives.

The Crown was not happy with this outcome, however. The British responded by passing new laws. As a direct result of this election, of the 137 proposals that Parliament voted on, 47 were intended to correct problems in Scotland and Ireland.

One of these was called "The Provisions for the Poor." It was popular, although a certain clause in the act called for realigning wealth for the creation of a fund to be managed by the Crown. The proceeds would be spent on the poor. This act was introduced for a specific reason. It had been designed by Orson Peterson to legally take all Delaney holdings.

The Delaneys were the first family to which the law would be applied. It later became known as "The Poor Removal Act." Plans were being made to foreclose on all the businesses and to take their estate. This case was a model that later would be used across Ireland. Conway himself would be the temporary steward until the crown awarded an officially designated Lord (which meant whomever the Queen wanted to reward.) This new Duke would be the owner of the land that had been in the hands of this Irish family for generations. The Delaneys would soon be considered squatters, subject to removal.

The Delaneys were not to find out what was happening until it was too late, but nothing went on in the western part of Ireland that Mickey Delaney didn't know about. It was Danny O'Connell who discovered the plot. He overheard William bragging about how that harlot who was living with the Irish would soon come running home to him when they lost all their land. Then he would teach her some respect. After doing some checking around, he discovered what Conway was planning.

Mickey told Molly what the Brits were up to. They decided to keep it quiet until after the wedding. The wedding went off this time without a problem. Patrick and Lucinda traveled together to a remote cottage on an island north of Donegal to begin their married life. The plan was for them to remain there until spring. Lucy and Patrick were as happy as any two young lovers could be. Their past troubles were behind them now. What was before them was a bright future together.

Danny O'Connell was as happy as he had been in years since he had finally obtained permission to take care of William for good. He smiled to himself as he saw William come out of a bar late one evening. Maybe he was headed home, or maybe he planned to go to another bar. Wherever he was going, it was certain that he would not arrive. Danny walked up behind him, stuck his long knife into his side, and twisted the blade. William screamed but nobody was around. William bled out on the street, then Danny dragged him to the river and rolled the limp body into the cold waters of the Shannon. Danny rode to the Delaney house to report the events of the night to Mickey.

CHAPTER 11

The Search

The next morning at daylight, William's body was found floating down the river. Had he not been seen by a fisherman, he would have made it out to sea, never to be found. Thomas Conway knew the Delaneys were behind it, but he wanted proof. If he couldn't find any then he would need to fabricate evidence. Every detective in the region was charged with finding out who had killed his son.

Abigail Conway arrived in Galway a few days later. She was demanding that justice be done. Her beloved son was gone. Conway knew she couldn't stand the boy. He also knew she would put on the biggest mourning act that Galway had ever seen.

"What exactly are you doing to find the killer of our son?" Mrs. Conway demanded of her husband.

"You know I can't discuss official police business with you," he said.

She had been asking the same thing for three days. His detectives had found little. The local snitches seemed to know nothing. A couple of them were prepared to say whatever they needed to if the money was right. Thomas would do that if he had to, but for now, he wanted to find real evidence.

"Am I supposed to accept that? It's like you don't even care. You never did care for him. That is why he's dead. You never were the kind of father you needed to be."

She was getting on his nerves. Thomas was ready to ship her back to London.

"Look at you," she continued. "You brought him to this backward place, where law and order are treated as a choice rather than a requirement."

"I remember you sending him," he snarled.

Thomas was getting tired of his complaining wife. She had done nothing but cause trouble since she got here. Half of Patel's people were ready to go back to India.

"Maybe I thought the great Thomas Conway could do what he has been asked to do. Establish order. Is that not what you got the award for? Look at you. Sitting in a nice office while the killer of our only child is parading around free. Right here under your nose."

"That's enough," Thomas said.

"No, it is not nearly enough. If you don't have someone arrested by tomorrow, you will find out what enough is," she turned and marched out of his office.

Good, he thought, maybe he would not have to see her again until tomorrow. He was suddenly missing Maggie.

"Simpson," he called.

His lieutenant came in and nodded.

"Please have every detective working on the Conway murder compile all their results and be in my office by the close of day."

Far to the north, Patrick and his bride were enjoying the tiny cottage overlooking the rocky Irish coastline. They had nothing to do but make love and take walks on the beautiful cliffs. Patrick had never been happier. Lucy seemed to have put all her troubles behind her as she gave him her unconditional affection. Arrangements had been made for them to remain there, isolated from the world.

The honeymooners had no idea William was dead. They knew nothing about their family fortunes being in jeopardy. Mickey had arranged for provisions to be delivered to them twice a week, so they did not need to go out. Everything was perfect.

At Delaney's home, Mickey sat with his old friend Finnegan talking openly about the new law. Finnegan was getting weaker by the day. He was so weak now he could not care for himself. Molly spent most of her time nursing him. He continued to shrink with every passing day. They all knew he would die soon. His mind remained sharp as he and Mickey talked about the latest developments, though.

Mickey considered him to be the wisest counsel available on any important issues. Mickey was thankful Finnegan was still alive. He would hate to face this upcoming decision without his friend's wisdom.

"Mick, there comes a time in most men's lives when they need to recognize what they are up against. You need to cut your losses. Get out when you can with whatever you can," Finnegan said.

"What are you saying?" Mickey asked.

"I'm saying legally they already own your land. Right or wrong they have the law on their side. They can take it whenever they want it. What they want now is for you to give them a good reason to take your life with all your possessions. What you have is of great value, but it is not as valuable as yours and Molly's lives. Eventually, you will give them a reason. I know your temper."

"Do I simply walk away from this? This is against everything I stand for. Where will I go? This is my country, not theirs. I will die defending it if I must."

"Yes, you will die. And they will get the land. Then what. What will Molly do? What will your daughters do? How will your boys react? Will they too sacrifice their lives for a lost cause, just to honor their Father and his pride?"

"You know you are the only man who would dare talk with me this way," Mickey said.

"When I was younger, I could have walked away. I should have walked away but I didn't, and it cost me my life. I would have died in that prison had you not rescued me. I went on to live a good life…"

A coughing spell interrupted him. After a moment he went on.

"…but I never got my vengeance. I learned you can live without it. I don't think you will be as fortunate as I was. There is nobody that can come to rescue you. I wish there were. No, my friend. They will kill you. So, give up the vengeance now, while you can."

Finnegan's voice was becoming weaker, but his eyes were clear.

"I'll think on it," Mickey said.

"You do that. Now I am going to sleep. I'm tired. Arguing with you makes me tired,"

He grinned, squeezed Mickey's hand, and closed his eyes.

Mickey sat watching his friend sleep. His breathing was shallow, and slower. He sat there for a few more hours, then climbed into bed with Molly. He told her everything Finnegan said before they both dropped off to sleep.

The next morning, when Molly went to check on Finnegan, she found him dead. The last words he had spoken were to tell her husband what he should do. She took that as a direct message from God. She was convinced that Mickey should do just as Finnegan had said. It went against everything that Mickey stood for, and yet he knew his friend was right. The Delaneys made up their minds that morning as they tended to the dead body of their dear friend and kinsman.

One interesting thing came out of the detectives' investigation. After some planning and plotting, it all fell into place. Conway sent a message to his wife that she need not come to his office today to harass him. By the end of the day, an arrest warrant would be issued with solid evidence that would convict the murderer of their son.

He was hoping the note worked because he was growing weary of her. He was ready to wrap this whole thing up so she would go back to London. Thinking about his spouse made him miss Maggie even more. He had not been able to find her anywhere. Another reason to hate the Delaneys.

Detective Smith had located a man hiding from the Delaneys—a man named Roger O'Malley. O'Malley, who had worked with the Delaneys for years, had been a confidential informant for the Crown for several months. He was eager to put an end to the Delaneys before they found him and put an end to him. Detective Smith was working with him on his story. He would be in Conway's office by noon today, ready to say what they wanted to hear. He would say that Sean Delaney had confessed to killing William Conway and dumping him in the river.

Conway figured this, along with the seizure of their land, would be what he needed to spring the trap he had set. His patience had paid off. The timing was perfect.

"Now son, tell me exactly what you know. Speak clearly and slowly because Simpson here will be recording your every word,"

"It was the night of July 17, 1856, right before dawn, when Sean Delaney came to where we were staying. He was bloody and disheveled. He told me he had killed William Conway. He followed him and stabbed him, then threw him in the river."

"He told you this exact thing?"

"Yes sir, that's what he told me."

"Did he say why he did this?"

"He didn't need to tell me. I knew he was looking for William Conway. He had planned to kill him. We all knew he would do it."

"Why did he want to kill William?" asked Conway.

"Because Lucinda might want to leave Patrick if William were available,"

"Are you saying Lucinda Conway is being held against her will?"

"Yes."

"Simpson please add kidnapping to the charge and include another Delaney in it. Patrick, I believe, is his name. Please continue."

"That's about it. He killed him, then he cleaned up and went to sleep. I have not seen him since that morning."

"Thank you very much, young man. You have been most helpful."

After Roger O'Malley left the room, Conway, Smith, and Simpson finished the paperwork, then shared a glass of brandy. As far as Conway was concerned, it was a day to celebrate.

The Delaneys met in the rain and cold to say goodbye to Finnegan. Earlier Mickey and Molly had told their boys about the loss of their home. Mickey did not share all the details—only that it was over. He shared with them their plans. As soon as the funeral was over, Mickey and Daniel left to tell Patrick and Lucinda the news. The rest of them would pack what they could carry in the wagons. They would leave for Belfast as soon as they could.

Each son dealt with the bad news in his own way. Danny was dazed and did not believe it was happening. John was confused. He could not understand why his father would walk away from a fight—a fight where they were clearly in the right. Sean said nothing. A sadness fell over him that was frightening. He had lost his best friend, he had lost Finnegan, and now they were losing their home—a home that had been in the Delaney family for generations. Michael experienced only fury. He was a volcano about to erupt.

Molly was worried about them all. She didn't even have time to mourn properly for Finnegan. Holding the family together was going to be the hardest thing she had ever done. She prayed that she could do it. It was so unfair. The last year they had on their land had been so pleasant. Now it was gone forever.

When Mickey arrived on the island, he found the cottage empty. It was small but very cozy and Lucy had fixed it up nicely. He looked around the cottage, then fixed himself a pot of coffee and settled in. It was a small island. He knew they would soon be back.

Patrick and Lucy were sitting bundled up in a blanket at their favorite spot. The wind was harsh, but they didn't care. They loved this place. It was where they would go to spend the evening watching the sunset over the water. The colors were magnificent. They eventually made their way back to the cottage where they found Mickey waiting.

"It is so good to see you," Lucy said, as she hugged Mickey and kissed his bearded face.

"I can see you two have been busy," he said looking at the bump in her belly that told him he would soon be a grandfather.

Lucy laughed.

"What brings you here?" Patrick asked.

He knew his father well enough to know he would not stop by just to see if his wife was pregnant.

"Get some coffee," he pointed at the pot on the stove. "Sit down. I have something to tell you."

They sat at the table together as Mickey told them about Finnegan's passing. He told them about the new law and that their land no longer belonged to them. There was no legal action that would change it. He told them the family was moving out as soon as possible.

Patrick could not hear any sadness or defeat present in his father's voice. He could, however, hear the usual confident tone that was always present when he instructed his men before battle. The attitude was that the Delaneys, if they stayed the course, would eventually be victorious.

A storm blew up a few minutes before dark on the second day after the Delaneys left the Island. Danny had now joined them. The temperature was dropping fast, and the rain was so fierce they could not keep a fire. Patrick and Danny made a shelter under the wagon with tarps on three sides. Lucy was wet and chilled but she never complained. Mickey rode to find a place they could shelter until the storm passed. It looked like a bad one that might last a while.

A few hours east of them he found a small farmhouse. The man there said they were welcome to stay. Mickey hurried back, gathered them, and they began the slow trip through the awful weather. The gale force winds with the thunder and lightning were making the horses skittish. Danny was able to keep them calm and moving through the mud as Patrick cared for his wife. It took four hours to get to the farm. The old couple had a place inside for Lucy to dry off and get warm. The men rode out the storm in the barn.

CHAPTER 12

Leaving Their Home

Conway was not pleased when he arrived at the Delaney house and found they had evacuated. They were taking the joy out of it for him. He had dreamed of watching them tearfully pack a few items under the watchful eye of his police. He settled in with about a dozen of his men and sent the rest to find the fugitive and bring him back to stand trial. Then justice would be done.

The Delaneys were headed northeast, moving along at a slow pace. Molly, Michael, Sean, John, and the girls were traveling with five of Mickey's men. One man rode in advance of the group, and another. observed from the rear. They were expecting the Brits. They had two loaded wagons and they were herding a few dozen sheep, a couple of milk cows, and fourteen horses, besides what they could ride. They would be easy to find. It was the morning of their third day when their man reported that the British posse was behind them. Michael, Sean, John, and three others rode to meet them. They exchanged a cordial greeting, then the officer in charge produced a document that said both Sean and Patrick were needed in Galway to assist in an official inquiry.

There were too many of them to disagree, so Michael decided they needed to see what this was all about. He told the men that Patrick was not with them, but Sean would be happy to assist them with their inquiry. He turned to John and said in Gaelic.

"John, I need you to take one man with you and continue to Belfast. Mother knows who to see when you arrive. Don't waste any time. Get them there as soon as you can."

"I can do that," John said.

Looking at the men, John knew they were fighters. He was sure Michael was aware of this too. John rode as fast as he could. A man named Clyde, who had been with the Delaneys for years, went with him. John did as instructed and got to them in a hurry. He found time later, while they were stopped to tell his mother what was going on. He could see the fear in her eyes.

About an hour had passed on their return trip to their previous home when the officer lifted his hand. Every soldier drew his weapon. Michael, Sean, and the other men with them did not make a move.

"What is this?" Michael asked. "There is no need for this."

The captain made another gesture and all the soldiers proceeded in disarming them.

"Why are you treating us like criminals?" Michael demanded.

"There is a good reason we are treating you like criminals. One of you is a criminal. And there is no reason for you to speak that backward dialect."

He had spoken to them in perfect Gaelic. The party rode on toward the Delaneys' previous home without saying another word.

When they arrived, they found Thomas Conway in a foul mood. He was put out because he had waited so long for his men to return, and they only had Sean. He informed them that Sean was going to be tried for the murder of his son. And he looked forward to justice, to see Sean's execution. Michael was certain that everything had already been decided. No amount of pleading their case made any difference. It did not matter to Conway that Sean had not been to Galway for months.

Sean read the charges. When he read that Roger had accused him, he hung his head.

Later that afternoon, Michael and the two men he had with him walked away from the group. They had Sean in chains by then. Michael sent the men he had with him to find his father and tell him what was happening.

As they rode to Galway, Michael tried to cheer Sean up, but it was useless. Emotionally and mentally, Sean was already dead. His world was gone. Michael's anger was growing with every breath he took. Conway would personally pay for this.

The same storm Patrick and company had weathered had now made it south to where John, Molly, and their party were camped. The wind was fierce, and the rain was coming down in buckets. John had also been unable to keep a fire going. They too made a shelter under the wagons to protect the girls, but it did not keep them dry. The wind was blowing in some frigid temperatures. The water on the ground was rising and they soon found themselves in a foot of icy water.

Six hours straight the wind and the rain pommeled them. The hardest part stopped after dawn. The rain was still coming down as the north wind blew in colder than before. Everything they had was wet. As soon as it was light enough to see, Clyde and John assessed the damage. It was not good. It took John several hours to make a fire, it was almost impossible to keep the fire going, but somehow, they managed. Clyde was able to find some of the animals. Half the sheep were gone, never to be seen again, but he found the horses and the cows.

By noon, they were able to start drying out their clothes. The many hours that Molly and the girls remained in wet cold clothing had taken a toll. They would not be able to travel again for several days. Clyde butchered a calf injured in the storm so they had meat to eat, if little else.

Through the whole ordeal, John had proven himself a man upon whom they could rely. He cared for his family and got them moving again as soon as possible. By the time they reached Belfast, Molly and the girls had begun to rally.

It was troubling that Mickey and the rest of the family had not arrived. They should have been here several days before. John, Clyde, and the girls had farther to travel. They had lost several days and had left after Mickey. John was worried.

After the storm, Lucy began to hemorrhage. The old gentleman that owned the farm went for a doctor as his wife cared for Lucy. The doctor arrived and told them she had not lost the baby but could not be moved. The bleeding had stopped but she was very weak. Mickey and Daniel helped the farmer while Patrick and the man's wife cared for Lucy day and night. Finally, Mickey sent Daniel to Belfast to see about the others and tell them about Lucy.

When Conway and his posse reached Galway, they placed Sean in jail. Sean had not said a word and would not eat anything. Michael found a lawyer to represent his brother but there was nothing he could do. The police had all the facts in their favor. It did not matter that it was all contrived.

The trial was set for the sixth day after their return. A speedy trial with a guilty verdict should send the message Conway wanted. Abigail was pleased with the outcome and was planning to return to London as soon as she witnessed justice with her own eyes.

Michael kept himself busy trying to get Sean released. It was soon evident that it was useless. Neither he nor the lawyer could alter the outcome. After a few days, he decided to plan his next move. He sent a message to Belfast to report the latest news about Sean to his father. Then he selected six men he could trust to help him. There were over a hundred men in the area he could call upon. For what he planned, six would be enough.

Word reached Belfast about Sean's trial the day before it was scheduled to begin. As Molly read the note she wept bitterly. She would not be there for her precious Sean. To make things even worse, she still had no idea if the rest of the family was safe. There had been no word from Mickey and she was beginning to fear the worst. When she thought it could not get any worse, Danny arrived with the news about Lucy. Early the next morning, she and Danny left for the farmhouse. It was too late to save her precious Sean but perhaps she could save Lucy.

Michael and his six comrades sat silently in the courtroom as officers marched Sean into court in chains. He had lost weight and he looked ill. Michael thought maybe he would die before they killed him. The judge was a young man who showed little interest in the procedure. Michael could tell by the way he kept looking toward Conway that his entire interest was in pleasing the police chief.

The well-organized evidence was presented methodically. The lawyer for Sean did his best to dispute the official finding, but the case was too compelling. When Roger O'Malley testified, Sean looked up at him. It was the only time he lifted his head. Michael saw tears run down Sean's face as his best friend betrayed him.

After several hours, the judge pronounced the sentence. It was as they expected. The only surprise was the method of execution. Sean was to be "Blown from a Gun." The date was set at dawn, three days from the court day.

Michael had no idea what this type of execution entailed. Later that day, he found a policeman who told him about it. It was the cruelest method of execution the British had ever conceived. They had learned it from the Mongols. This was to be the first time this sentence had been executed in the British Isles. Conway had seen it done a few times in India and he knew it to be an effective method to horrify the crowd. It was a lesson these people needed to learn.

The convicted prisoner would be tied to the end of a cannon. As it was fired, it produced the most horrible spectacle. The head typically flew the greatest distance with all the other body parts sprayed across the field. The policeman explaining it to Michael seemed to be looking forward to seeing it done in person. He had only heard of it.

Danny and his mother arrived at the farmhouse and told Mickey about Sean. Mickey left immediately by himself for Galway. He had no idea what he would find when he arrived.

The ferry was halfway across the River Shannon when Roger O'Malley, who was trying to get out of town before the execution, got a strange feeling that something was not right. There were not as many passengers as there should have been on the boat at this time of day. The old man who usually ran the ferry was not there and the man that operated it looked familiar. Roger could not place him though it was too late to do anything about it now. He put his hand on his knife and scanned the few others on board.

Minutes later, he heard the sound of a pistol being cocked, and he heard a voice.

"Enjoy your last breath, you lying traitor."

That is when it dawned on him who these men were. They all worked for the Delaneys. Danny O'Connell pulled the trigger, gratified as the slug entered Roger's right ear and exited the left, taking with it a good portion of the brain matter in Roger's head. His pockets were then filled with stones and his body was dumped into the current, which would be Roger O'Malley's final resting place.

The men paid the old ferryboat captain, then hurried back to find Michael. They were worried he would not hold it together long enough to carry out their plans. At this stage, nothing was more important than their success.

CHAPTER 13

Death of a Son

On the day Sean Delaney was to be executed, a large crowd assembled in an emerald-green pasture just east of the River Shannon. It was a beautiful morning. A cannon was pulled to the valley by a team of parade-quality horses. All of Conway's people were in dress uniform. They made quite a spectacle of transporting both the prisoner as well as the gun. The entire ordeal would only last a few seconds, so Conway took all the time he needed to make sure the execution would be remembered as a momentous occasion. It was two hours past dawn, and they were still waiting as more people arrived. Few people even knew who Sean Delaney was. Curiosity was drawing them. Later, most would regret having seen it.

When Conway was finally satisfied there was a large enough crowd, he nodded to an officer in full dress uniform. The man stepped forward and read aloud the charges. While he was reading, two other policemen were removing Sean's chains. Then they attached a leather strap tightly around his ankles. More straps were used to tie each wrist to the wheels of the cart. When the reading of the charges concluded and Sean was attached properly a few inches from the ten-inch gun barrel, the men marched behind the cannon, Conway drew his polished sword and raised it high into the air. Raw rage filled Michael. The police chief would pay dearly for this. Sean looked toward the sky and mumbled a few words for the first time since being arrested.

Conway dropped the sword as two policemen swung their swords toward the wheel to cut the leather straps. Another man placed a burning torch at the base of the cannon. The fuse sizzled for an instant, then the loud boom of the gun displaced the silence. Dark smoke billowed from the barrel of the gun as Sean's body was blown into pieces all over the field. The gun had done its work as expected. Sean's head rose about thirty feet in the air and landed in the field among the other limbs and body parts.

A collective gasp was heard from the crowd. Then they dispersed, hoping they would be able to forget what they had seen. Conway grinned at the people's response, pleased with what he saw. These people would soon spread the word and everyone in the region would fear him. He had won.

A celebration party was planned for that evening at Conway's house. Thomas took off the rest of the day to help Abigail prepare for their guests. With the execution out of the way, he was hoping it was the last time he would have to deal with her for a while. She would soon return to London to take up her rightful place as the biggest gossip in the city.

Michael's men had brought with them a wooden box that would serve as Sean's casket. They went over the field with a much reverence as they could muster, gathering as much of Sean as they could find. Michael sat quietly, watching his brother's remains being placed in the coffin. A tall, stately Indian man approached him. He bowed his head and spoke with a heavy accent.

"Your brother Patrick. He is a good man. I also know that this brother," he pointed towards the field, "was an innocent man."

"How do you know this?" Patrick asked.

"My name is Kanji Patel and I work for Thomas Conway. I have been with him for many years. I run his house. I know about everything that goes on there."

"Please continue," Michael said.

"It is not important how I know this. What I came to tell you is that Mr. Conway has already issued orders to arrest everyone in your family except your two young sisters." He turned to leave.

"Wait a minute," Michael said. "Why are you telling me this?"

"I told you I know your brother Patrick and he is a good man. He does not deserve this. I know little about you, but I suspect you do not deserve this either."

Patel looked on sadly as the men continued to gather Sean's remains. Then he walked away.

Lucy was not getting worse, but she was not any better. They decided it would be better if she could stay at the farmhouse rather than risk a journey to Belfast. Molly and Patrick alternated staying by her side, trying to encourage her, willing her back to health.

Michael and his six chosen men met after Sean's remains were tended to properly. Roger O'Malley had been dealt with and there were a few more scores to settle, but Michael needed to bring Mickey up to date first. He spent the next hour composing a letter.

Father,

> *I am writing this to inform you of events that have happened or will happen soon. I have also discovered more plots the Tans have to kill us all. They are smug because they have the law on their side. Just after you left to see Patrick, the police caught up with us and they took Sean. We could do nothing except ensure that Mother and the girls got away safely. I am still in Galway, where I witnessed Sean's completely unjust trial and execution. It was a bloody mess. I am glad no one else from the family was here. I will repay the debt. Blood for blood.*

I have all I need to do this. Afterward, if I can get away, which is doubtful, I will meet you and the rest of the family in Belfast. Patrick and his wife will come too, as soon as she can travel, probably after the baby is born. Danny is with Mother and the girls. It was Roger O'Malley who betrayed us. He has been taken care of. John should be in Belfast soon as well.

Keep the Faith,
Your son,
Michael

"Make sure my father gets this," he told Elias Clemons.

Elias was a trusted man who had been with the Delaneys for years. He knew Mickey as well as anyone. Elias would know how to find him if anyone did.

"No one else is to see this. Is that clear? I have no idea where he is —probably in Belfast—but he might be anywhere. Get several other men to help you if you need them. You are the only one that can give him this. It is vital. Do you understand? Take as many men as you need, but get it to him as soon as you can."

"Aye I, I can do it," Elias said.

He took the note and immediately left to recruit helpers. When he was gone Michael continued with the five that were left.

"The time is now men," he said. "It must go down tonight. Everyone will be at Conway's home. There are two entrances to the house. Three of us will take the front, and three will take the rear. You all know who we need to find. Are there any questions?"

"Yes, we usually have backup plans if things don't go well. What is the plan?" Danny O'Connell asked.

"Danny, we have none. We do it as planned. There is no tomorrow. I will be honest with you. We may not come away from this one. If anyone wants to leave, do it now."

He looked at each man. They were all in. They had seen what Conway had done to Sean. All of them were ready to exact the revenge that was due.

Meanwhile, a man named Joseph Porter found Mickey Delaney in a town called Longford. He was on his way to Galway and did not want to delay. The man told him that Michael was trying to get an urgent message to him. He also told him it was too late for Sean. He had been executed. He did not give him any more details about it. Porter sent someone to find Elias Clemons.

While they waited for Elias, Mickey had time to reflect on the news of Sean's death. He went off by himself and wept bitterly. He was devastated. He had lost men before, and it was never easy. But this was different. He knew what it would do to Molly and that troubled Mickey even more than his own grief.

As Mickey reflected upon Sean's life, he sunk into a deep depression. He berated himself for having led his son into a life that would result in this—a brutal death before he had time to experience the joys that life had for him. Most of Sean's life had been hard. He never had a real childhood. He had begun fighting with his father and brothers at such an early age. All these thoughts and emotions rendered Mickey helpless with grief over his loss.

Thomas Conway, however, was in a jubilant mood as he welcomed his guests. After a sumptuous meal, they would toast their victory. The conflict was over. Abigail was there mixing with the local dignitaries. Everyone of any importance would be in attendance. This was what Abigail lived for. She would shed a few tears for her beloved son and then toast the just verdict. The bloody mess on the field had not affected her at all. She had talked about it all day with the staff.

As preparation for the festivities continued, there was another set of preparations underway. Barney McCormick was a Scotsman who had lived his entire life in Belfast. His family had been forced to leave his native land, so he hated the British as much as any Irishman. This made him a natural ally for the Delaneys. He owned a successful ship-building company and did business with several companies Mickey had started. When he found out what had happened to them, he visited Molly, John, and the girls.

When John explained the difficulties Lucinda and Patrick were facing, Barney offered his assistance. Knowing all that the Delaneys had done for Ireland, he was moved by their sacrifice and he wanted to help them.

When he arrived in Cookstown, Barney found Lucinda to be charming and gracious, though she was still quite weak from her illness. Barney was also moved by the attention her adoring Patrick paid her. Barney was an influential man in the area and he quickly arranged to purchase the farm where they were staying. The farmer and his wife were pleased to relocate to a farm near her sister who was getting older and needed their help. Barney also paid a local doctor handsomely to pay regular visits to Delaneys' new home.

All this was unknown to Thomas Conway, however, as he continued with the preparations for his victory dinner. Several modifications were being made to his home to accommodate the evening's expected crowd. As part of this, the dining room doors and the doors to the parlor had been removed to create a larger area so that all the guests could hear the speeches and toasts he was planning.

The elaborate feast would be a rousing success, carefully calculated so that when the time came for speeches and toasts, the mood in the room would be electric. Several guests would extol Abigail Conway's strength in the face of her son's death. Others would recount young William's promising future, cut short by violent tragedy. The keynote speaker would be Lieutenant Simpson, who would wrap up the speeches with a recap of how the Irish problem had been resolved. His speech would include highlights of Conway's long and illustrious career. Particular emphasis would be placed on Conway's advanced knowledge of criminology and how this would transform police work all over the Empire.

Also unknown to Conway was the ease with which Michael Delaney would obtain all the information he needed about the arrangement of the rooms, the planned events of the evening, and the expected guests. Nor did he imagine that removing the doors to the dining room and parlor would work in the rebels' favor. Secure in his belief that he had now defeated the Delaneys, the celebrated criminologist never once entertained the thought that they might still take their revenge.

CHAPTER 14

Revenge

As the speeches began, Michael and his men moved into position outside the Conway house. They were confident about the layout of the interior, and as they expected, there were half a dozen guards at each gate. The distance between the gates and the house was about forty paces in the rear and sixty-five in the front. It didn't matter how many men were guarding the house, though. Michael and his men were going in. The horror of seeing Sean blown to pieces that morning had made their blood boil. They planned to take out the guards as quietly as possible, then storm the house, going room to room until all the targets were eliminated. Then they would fight their way out, if they were still alive. Survival was not their primary concern. Vengeance was their priority.

Michael had two men with him, and they planned to take the front gate. Danny O'Connell had the other two with him. All were experienced warriors. They were hiding in the bushes nearby. They had been there two hours waiting for the right time. A young Irishman who worked in the Conway kitchen signaled to Michael at the same time an Irish maid signaled Danny. The covey was in the trap. The well-fed group was now crowded into the ballroom, drawing room, and library. With the doors removed, these rooms became a makeshift auditorium perfect for the tribute to Conway. The layout was also perfect for revenge. There were few entry and exit points. Michael and his men were poised to attack.

The celebration inside was growing more boisterous. Liquor flowed freely and it was clear the guests were having a wonderful time. The first action occurred when a soldier strolled outside toward the bushes to relieve himself. He was unbuttoning his trousers when he felt something behind him. Before he could turn to see, a knife blade flashed before his eyes. He reached for his throat reflexively but it was too late. Warm liquid saturated both hands. He looked at them and tried to scream, but nothing came out. He dropped to his knees and within a few seconds, he was gone. The killing had been soundless.

Michael's man Donald dragged him deeper into the bushes and then returned to where Michael and Joseph were crouching. He winked at them. One down.

The second step in the plan occurred when a guard came looking for his buddy. Donald slipped up behind him. This man was more cautious. He spun around before Donald was close enough to attack. The man used his rifle to club Donald across the face. Donald went down. The guard was on him immediately and his heavy boot landed square on Donald's face. Donald would never move again. The guard bent over to see who he had stomped when Joseph's club connected with the man's head. He too was finished. Michael and Joseph dragged both bodies into the bushes. Now they were down to two men in the front.

In the rear, Danny and his men had killed four guards without incident. There were only three guards left. One turned to enter the house. As soon as the man was out of sight, Danny and his men rushed the last two and killed them. The fight was difficult but quick. Danny was cut badly above his right eye, but he wiped off the blood and continued the fight.

Michael and Joseph rushed to the front door. A shot rang out from the rear of the house. It had struck the man to Danny's left and he went down. As all attention focused momentarily on the rear exit, Michael and Joseph capitalized on their advantage as Conway's men were distracted.

The soldier who had shot at Danny's group was now preparing to shoot again. He drew his pistol and fired, this time hitting nothing. The man to the left of Danny fired his long gun and killed the shooter. The guard fired another shot toward the ground as he went down. The alarm was sounded. Everyone now knew they were under attack.

As soon as Michael and Joseph heard the shots, they opened fire. They killed the first two easily. The last man was more trouble. He found cover and began firing back. Joseph was able to get a clean shot at him and dispatched him before he caused them too much delay. They were now ready to enter the house. They needed to reload, but there was no time.

Simpson was in the middle of his speech when they heard the shots. Conway figured it was nothing to worry about and he nodded for Simpson to continue. He was aggravated at the timing. Nobody was paying enough attention as they all looked around mumbling and speculating as to what the shots were all about. Conway rose from his seat.

"There is nothing to be alarmed about," he said.

He nodded at a soldier by the door to go check things out.

"Please continue, Mr. Simpson."

The soldier opened the front door and found Michael standing there. He was out of breath but was still able to drive a long knife through the man's midsection. He pushed him aside. Joseph arrived seconds later and they entered the celebration together. The crowd was now in full-blown panic. Women were screaming as the guests trampled each other in their attempts to seek safety from the Irish assassins.

Michael dropped his rifle and with a pistol in each hand, began shooting every man in uniform he could see. Joseph was doing the same thing as they moved forward, firing one shot after another.

Thomas Conway suddenly knew the extent of his miscalculation. It was every man for himself. Abigail was trying to exit through the kitchen. The door was jammed with others trying to do likewise. Shots were heard in the kitchen as well.

Danny O'Connell and his man James had entered the back door. They had taken up positions in the kitchen, sorting through the crowd, shooting guards, and ushering servants out the back door. Danny now was working his way up the hall from the rear. There was blood everywhere and the effect was exactly what Michael had hoped for. The chaos prevented any sort of organized resistance. A few of Conway's soldiers had side arms and were shooting back. This only added bullets to the mix. The sound of lead ricocheting off the walls further enhanced the nightmarish scene.

Michael had not been able to locate Conway. He continued to reload and shoot as he searched each room. Joseph took a bullet in the gut. He doubled over in pain and went to his knees, but immediately reloaded and then continued firing from a kneeling position.

Abigail had fainted from the drama. She was a large woman and she had picked the absolute worse place to go down. Her body was blocking the exit. Several maids trying to get her to freedom had ended up wedging her further into the threshold of the door, eliminating that as an exit. With no one else coming through the kitchen, James could now join Danny in the hall.

Conway had made it to the servant's hallway and was going up the back stairway. Danny saw him and followed. At the same time, a volley of bullets from the soldiers blasted through the back hallway, killing James and several guests. Help had arrived. Michael saw Danny run up the stairs. He hoped he was chasing Conway. Michael fought his way up the main stairway. From his new location, he now had the advantage. He was shooting down on the soldiers as they rushed in.

Many died before they stopped coming.

Conway ran into his bedroom. His service revolver was on the nightstand, loaded and ready to use. Danny came through the door as Conway swung around and fired. The shot went through Danny's right arm. Conway grinned and cocked the pistol again. Danny was upon him before he could get off another shot. He tackled Conway and they landed in a heap on the rug by the bed. Danny was on top of Conway with his knife to the man's throat.

"Where is that grin now?" Danny asked.

Conway's eyes widened.

"It's better this way. I'll cut you like I did your boy. That's right I'm the one who killed that little pig. Now it's your turn."

Danny slit his throat, then stabbed the old man in the gut, dragging the blade up until he hit the bone of his rib cage.

Conway grunted. It was over. Danny got up as Michael rushed in. He arrived in time to see Conway take his last breath.

"Sorry I couldn't wait for you, lad," Danny said.

"Let's get out of here."

Danny was losing blood fast. When they reached the stairs, they faced several soldiers ready to fire. Michael lifted his pistol and squeezed off one last shot before the men opened fire and dropped Danny and Michael. They would die shoulder to shoulder, like the valiant warriors they were.

"We did it mate," whispered Michael.

Danny grinned as his eyes glazed over. Michael lay waiting for what he knew would come. A soldier's saber plunged into his chest. It was over. The Delaneys had exacted their revenge.

CHAPTER 15

Saying Goodbye

The Delaney family was finally reunited, at least what was left of them. The occasion was not a happy one. Molly and Patrick held each other as they stood over the graves of Michael, Sean, and Finnegan. Patrick was torn between grief over his brothers and concern for Lucinda. She had insisted he go to his mother.

As they left the cemetery, they knew it would be a long time before they returned if they ever did. They held each other and wept for their loss. Molly was in shock. The only thing that kept her going was her girls. She knew she had to be strong for them. She could not give up now, no matter how she felt.

Meanwhile, in Galway, there was another gathering. This one was not solemn. The British wanted their revenge. When word of the Conway massacre reached Peel, he was furious. Orders from Peel himself were dispatched to ensure that every Delaney was arrested and held accountable. Word of the family gathering had reached them and a group of six armed policemen were rapidly making their way to the cemetery. The plan was to arrest every Delaney at once, stage a quick trial, and then rid the region of these vermin.

A few miles from the cemetery, the policemen stopped at a creek to water their horses. As they mounted up, Delaney's men opened fire on them from three directions. The British never had a chance to return fire. All six lay dead. Delaney's men found the arrest papers on the soldiers and sent a rider to take them to Mickey. The rest of the men disposed of the bodies and confiscated the horses and guns. It would be several days before anyone knew what had happened to these lawmen.

Patrick left with three men as soon as the note arrived from the rider. The rest of the Delaneys, except John, headed towards Belfast. They had thirty-two armed warriors with them to accompany them and ensure their safety. Belfast was a large enough place that the Delaneys could blend in and hide from the authorities until they had time to arrange for passage out of Ireland. The arrest papers left little doubt in their minds that if the British got their hands on them, they would suffer Sean's fate.

Because few people knew John in Galway, he was chosen to slip into town for Wallace Conway. Patrick wanted him to be with his daughter. It was late when John arrived in Galway, and he soon discovered Wallace was no longer at his old address. John spent the rest of the night visiting pubs to see if anyone knew where he might be. In most places he went, someone knew Wallace but had not seen him in weeks. Finally, John found a man who knew how to find him. Wallace often frequented the Anglican Church in the evenings where soup would be served to the homeless. There was no shortage of homelessness in Ireland. The small bowl of soup was all that kept many of them alive. At daybreak. John found a livery stable where he slept with his horse. It was too dangerous to be on the streets in daylight.

That evening, John found Wallace in the soup line at the church. The man needed a meal and a bath. John took him out of the line and then checked him into a local hotel.

"I suppose you are wondering why I asked you to come with me," John said.

Wallace had cleaned up and they were eating a hearty bowl of lamb stew at the hotel.

"I would have gone with the devil himself to get a bath and a meal like this."

He had been sober for over a week, not because he wanted to be, but because he had no money and everyone he knew was tired of buying him whiskey. When Thomas Conway died, so had Wallace's position with the police department.

"I was sent here to tell you something," John said.

He looked around the room. Nobody seemed to be paying any attention to them.

"I am ready to hear what you say. I am also eager to spend the night in a real bed again. I thank you for your kindness. Please, tell me whatever you need to tell me."

"You must promise to not tell anyone," John said.

"My lips are sealed," Wallace replied.

For the first time, he was intrigued by what the young Irishman might say.

"My name is John Delaney. You know my brother Patrick."

"Yes, I do," he answered.

"He is married to your daughter. She is having a baby and is very ill and Patrick wanted you to know."

"Where is she?"

"You don't need to know. My family is being pursued by the authorities, as you may know, so we will soon be leaving Ireland. Patrick also wanted you to know this," John said.

John was ready to walk out. He had planned to tell Wallace Conway the news, then catch up with his family.

"Take me to see her," Wallace demanded.

"That is not possible."

"Please, she is all I have. I know I have not been the best father. I know I didn't do right by her, but I love her. She reminds me so much of her mother. It almost killed me when I lost my wife. I've lost everything. I can't lose her too. Please, I beg of you,"

John sat back down. For some strange reason, he felt pity for Wallace.

John slept with his horse again that night. He wasn't going to put his name on the hotel register. Before dawn. John woke Wallace, got him dressed, and tried to get him on the horse John had purchased. It was not easy. Wallace had never ridden a horse. John could not imagine a grown man who couldn't ride a horse. Wallace kept losing his balance and sliding off first one side, then the other. Wallace was making a spectacle of himself. John worried about the attention they were attracting. He had wanted to slip out unseen but this was more of a parade than a quick getaway.

When they were finally beyond the city limits, John left Wallace sitting in the shade of a tree while he doubled back to see if they were being followed. When he was satisfied, he returned and resumed the arduous task of situating Wallace atop a horse.

"Lucy, I need to tell you something," Patrick said.

He had ridden all night to reach her after he left the cemetery. Looking into her eyes seemed to refresh him and at the same time make him want to cry. If he could only carry her off somewhere away from all of this, he would do so.

"It's so good to hear your voice and see your sweet face."

She touched his cheek tenderly.

"They have issued arrest papers for my entire family,"

"They can't do that," she said. "How do you know?"

"We have seen the documents. My entire family will be leaving Ireland. I have no idea where we will end up."

"We will figure it out," she said.

If she were with him, she didn't care where they went.

"I am so sorry to have gotten you into a life like this. I should have never followed you back into the store that day. I should have left you alone. You would have had a good life without getting mixed up with the Delaneys."

"Patrick, you are the only good thing that has ever happened to me. I cannot imagine a life without you and your family. No matter where we go, I just need to be with you."

"I love you Lucy and I am so sorry your life has been turned upside down because of me."

"If I never have another good thing happen in my life the memories of the last few months of us together on the Island is all I'll ever need."

They embraced and kissed each other. A tear ran down Patrick's cheek as he held her.

"Do you speak French?" Patrick asked.

"Yes, I can, but I'm probably very rusty. Are we going to France?"

"I do not know where we will go. We must get you well first. Then after the baby comes, we will decide. I don't want you to worry about anything except getting well.

John and Wallace were far enough away from Galway now to feel at ease. John had spent much of the day repeatedly helping Wallace get back on his horse. The last couple of hours the man had done a better job staying on, but his whining about how the horse smelled and how rough the ride was had increased. They made camp and John fixed them something to eat while Wallace went on complaining about the travel conditions.

"Mr. Conway," John said, after listening to him whine about everything. "I'll be happy to take you back to Galway first thing in the morning."

"I can't go back there. I have nothing there."

There was an urgent panic in his voice.

"The horse you are riding is as gentle as they get. The weather is not too bad, and the road is smooth. Before we get to where we are going it will be quite a bit harder riding. Are you sure you want to go on?" John asked.

"Yes, I am sure," Wallace replied.

"Then relax and get some rest. We need to do better tomorrow than we did today."

John got up to gather some more wood for the fire. He was tired of his traveling companion. He loved Patrick and would do anything for him, but this task was turning into a nightmare.

The next morning it took a long time to get loaded and ready to leave. Wallace insisted on a second pot of coffee. He said he needed several cups of coffee in the morning to move his bowels. He finally decided it was time for his morning constitutional and he disappeared into the bushes. John had never heard such a cacophony in his life. He had seen men shot in the gut who made less noise. His mother didn't make that kind of noise when she was giving birth. Every so often John would ask how he was, afraid that maybe Wallace had expired. Wallace's replies were all more specific than John wanted to hear. In the end, he proclaimed success and he wanted to tell John all about it. John refused to listen. Wallace got up on his horse without help. It took several tries, but he did it. John hoped that perhaps things were improving though Wallace spent much of the day talking about how sore his tailbone was. John kept them moving and they made better time the second day.

Meanwhile, Mickey and the rest of the family were almost to Belfast when some of his men rode up and told them they must go toward the coast. The British were in the city looking for them. There was a cottage near the east coast where they would be safe. Daniel escorted them to the coast, then took a couple of men to check on Patrick. Molly was concerned about Lucy.

They settled into the cottage on the water the next afternoon. The girls found a little beach to play on while the adults conferred.

"Mulroney and I are going into Belfast in the morning," Mickey told Molly. "The men are camped out all around this place. You will be safe."

"Why are you going into Belfast?" she asked.

"I have business to take care of. Don't worry. I will stay clear of the police,"

"Do you promise?"

"Yes, I promise."

He kissed her as they held each other.

"I like it here," Molly said. "The girls do, too."

She looked out over the water.

"They are just ready to finally settle down somewhere," she added.

"This is good for now, but we will need to leave as soon as we can. I know these Brits; they will not give up until they find us.

They went to sleep holding each other.

The next day, Wallace's bowels were worse than the day before. After the same routine of groaning and cursing, they continued into the mountains. The travel conditions were worsening.

They had only made it a few miles when John stopped and made camp. There was a small town ahead and he was going there to get supplies. Wallace was happy to rest but the prospect of a nearby town initiated a brand-new category of complaint. This one had to do with him needing a drink. If he had but a few sips of whiskey the travel would be much better and his bowels would again operate as they should. When John agreed to get a bottle of whiskey, Wallace perked up.

He had no idea what the combination of whiskey and Wallace's bad bowels would produce. He got his answer the next morning when he found Wallace snuggled up to an empty bottle. The man had somehow gotten the bottle out of John's bags after he was asleep. He had promised John that he would only take one drink before bed, and one in the morning for his bowels. The bottle should have lasted the entire trip.

John could not rouse him until the afternoon. Wallace couldn't walk so there was no way he could ride. An entire day was wasted with John pouring coffee down Wallace as the man bemoaned the insufficiency of his plumbing.

The next morning, Wallace's bowels were working again and he was sober enough to ride. Once again headed north. The mountains were growing steeper with more elevation to come. John had no idea how he was going to get Wallace Conway through these mountains. But it was too late for him to go around them.

CHAPTER 16

Father and Daughter

The weather was holding and the trails were clear. Things were looking hopeful until Wallace's horse pulled up lame. John made camp, then rode ahead to find a town where he might find a horse to buy. John found a good horse at a fair price a few hours from camp. With any luck, they should reach the cottage in a few more days.

When he returned to the camp, he found everything as he had left it, but Wallace was gone. John figured he was again experiencing digestive issues and would return soon. After a few hours, he went out looking for Wallace. He found his tracks and followed them. The tracks seemed to be circling the camp.

Earlier that day, Wallace had wandered off for no real reason. He soon found he was lost, trapped on a narrow trail. He had slipped on loose gravel and tumbled down a steep ridge. He ended up on a big rock. He was scratched up, but not hurt. However, the rock was a ten-foot drop. There was nothing on his left or right, so the only way out was to climb the rock wall he had just slid down. He tried for several hours, then gave up. He sat down and cried. He would die here on the mountain and would never see his Lucy again.

John kept looking for him. It would be dark soon and the nights were cold this high up. The tracks were leading nowhere so there was little hope of finding him. John was beginning to worry that he had lost the old fool. Just when he thought about returning to the camp, he heard something. A faint grumbling. He followed the noise and looked down the ridge and saw what the noise was. Wallace Conway was about ten feet down, sound asleep on a big rock. His snoring had led John to him.

"That is a strange place to take a nap," John said.

Wallace woke with a start. He had cried himself to sleep.

"I can't climb up. I fell and now I'm stuck here on this rock."

"I can see that," John said.

"Can you get me out?"

"I might," John said. "I'm trying to figure out if I want to. You have been nothing but trouble the whole trip. I may leave you there."

You can't do that," Wallace whined. "Please, I won't cause you any more trouble, I promise."

"Go back to sleep, I need to think about this."

John left to get a rope. He could hear Wallace yelling and begging for mercy as he walked away.

Wallace was still whining when John returned. It was hard work, but John was able to get him back on the trail.

"How long had you been there?" John asked.

"Most of the day. I was just taking a walk…"

"I don't want to hear it," John interrupted. "You had no business wandering off. You might have killed yourself,"

Wallace was quiet the rest of the evening.

Daniel arrived at the cottage to find Patrick pacing back and forth. Lucinda had become ill in the night and he had gone to fetch the doctor. She had been fine when she went to bed. A few hours later she began throwing up violently. Her fever was high again and she was so weak she couldn't hold her head up.

Patrick and the doctor arrived around dawn and stayed with her throughout the morning.

"Tell me about her," Daniel asked later that day.

Patrick shook his head.

"She is not doing well," Patrick said, his voice trembling.

"What can I do?"

"I don't know what anyone can do. I hope the doctor can do something. He hasn't said a word."

Daniel sent one of his men for Molly. She would know what to do. He told the man to ride hard and bring her back as soon as he could.

Another hour passed and the doctor came out.

"She is resting now, or she is in a coma. I've done all I can. She will either make it or not. I'll stay with her and do whatever I can."

The Delaneys were having trouble staying together. The boys were scattered, each trying to reach increasingly tentative destinations. Mickey was in Belfast. He was helping organize a rally. Recently there had been trouble between the Catholics and the Protestants about jobs. The Catholics were tired of always having to take low-paying jobs while their Anglican neighbors got all the high-paying skilled jobs. Mickey had little to do with religion, but he knew injustice when he saw it. He was trying to keep a low profile.

He knew about the warrants against him and his family. His family was stretched out over half of Ireland. This worried him, though the British urgency to find them seemed to have waned. Politicians have a way of moving on. He had begun to hope that if they stayed out of sight for a while they might stay in their beloved Ireland.

When John and Wallace arrived at Patrick and Lucinda's cottage, they could tell something was wrong. A crowd of people had gathered outside. and Danny was coming out to meet them. John knew it didn't look good.

"How are you, Johnny?"

"What is wrong?" John asked.

"It's Lucy. She's not doing well."

"Where is Patrick?"

"Inside with Mother. The doctor said only a few people at a time could go in. Patrick and Mother are there now."

Lucy had finally come out of the coma, but she was very weak. She could not keep food down.

Daniel knocked on the door and told Patrick that John and Wallace Conway had arrived. A few minutes later, Patrick stepped out of the room.

"Did you have any trouble, John?" Patrick asked. "I was expecting you a couple of days ago."

"Yes, we had troubles. I'll tell you about it later," John said as he glared at Wallace.

"Mr. Conway I am so happy you could come. Lucy will be delighted to see you," Molly said.

She reached for John and pulled him into her, hugging and kissing him on the cheek. "You did great, Johnny. Thank you."

"How bad is she?" Wallace asked. "Can I see her?"

"Of course," Patrick said.

The doctor came out and Wallace went in alone to see her.

"Lucy darling, it's me," Wallace said.

Her eyes were closed, and she was perfectly still. She reached out her hand and he took it.

"Hello, Father," she said without opening her eyes.

Speaking seemed to take every ounce of strength she had.

"Lucy, I had no idea you were this ill."

"How could you know?"

She turned her head towards him and opened her eyes. They were not the clear, bright eyes he had seen all her life. She tried to smile.

"It is good to see you," she whispered.

"I am so sorry. If I could do something I would," Wallace said.

"Your being here is enough."

She closed her eyes again.

It wasn't long before she was asleep. Wallace hung his head and wept. His world was gone. Lucy was all he had, and now it looked as if she too, would leave him. After a few minutes, Patrick came in and Wallace left without saying a word. He was a broken man.

Patrick and Molly took turns sitting with Lucy the rest of the evening and into the night.

At dawn, Molly found John and Danny and told them she needed them to go to the girls. Molly said she would not leave Lucy again. John wanted to ask about the baby, but he didn't dare. He was afraid of the answer. He had never seen Patrick so sad. Before he left, he went in to see Lucy. Patrick had insisted.

"Lucy, it's John," he said.

"Hold my hand," she muttered softly.

He reached down and took her hand. She tried to squeeze it but had little strength.

"Thank you for bringing my father."

"It was no trouble," John lied.

"Patrick thinks the world of you, and so do I. You are growing into a fine man." She opened her eyes and looked at him. "Don't tell Patrick but I think you are the most handsome of the brothers."

She winked at him, then turned her head and closed her eyes. John held her hand a few minutes longer, then Danny went in to see her for a moment before they mounted up.

"I can never thank you enough for all you did for me," Wallace said as they left.

"Glad to do it," John lied again.

"I know I was a pain. Thank you,"

Patrick, Molly, and Wallace took turns sitting with Lucy. Each poured his heart out about how loved she was and how they wanted her to get well. She spent most of her time struggling to converse. The theme of every conversation was how much she loved her life now.

Wallace was a different man. He had spent most of his life worrying about what he wanted. Now all he cared about was what Lucy needed. He spent as much time as he could with her. Patrick was completely spent, however. He was glad his mother was here. While Wallace was with Lucy, Patrick poured his heart out to his mother, crying on her shoulder. They all knew that Lucy would soon leave them.

Danny and John found the girls as they expected. They were making the most of their situation. Their father had not returned, and nobody had heard from him. The girls missed their mother but understood she had to be with Lucy. They loved Lucy as everyone else did. Danny and John did not tell them how ill Lucy was

Danny sent a couple of men into Belfast to find their father. They also released about half their men. There was no need for a small army now. The place they were staying was out of the way. The British would not trouble them here.

Peel had not forgotten about the Delaneys. He had his detectives asking around in every city in Ireland. So far, they had not found anything. One report had them in Cork. Another reliable source said they were in Dublin. Others reported that they had crossed the channel and were in Scotland. Peel decided that these reports were a ruse designed to leave him frustrated enough to call off the search. There was not any chance of that. Peel was a determined man.

C H A P T E R 17

The Arrest

The demonstration was to be peaceful. It was meant to send a message that Catholics had a real grievance that needed to be heard. It turned ugly quickly when the police got involved, though. As usual, they took the side of the Anglicans and wasted no time escalating the conflict into a riot through the use of force. The Catholics fell back a few blocks and reorganized, then attacked again with weapons of their own—mostly clubs and knives. It got bloody in short order.

The fighting went on into the night with many casualties. Almost everyone involved was nursing some sort of wound. After dawn, more police showed up and the struggle was over. The rest of that day was spent caring for the wounded and grieving the loss of the fallen. The following day, the police went door to door, arresting whoever they thought was involved.

Mickey was nowhere near the fight, but he got swept up in the dragnet because he had been staying with a family that had been involved. The police had no idea who he was. He gave them a fake name and was hoping to be released.

West of Belfast, Lucy went into a coma soon after John and Danny left. She lived a few more days, then passed quietly into the next life. The last few hours were spent with Molly holding one hand and Patrick holding the other. Wallace sat silently at the foot of the bed, looking at her. Molly pronounced her gone and mother and son went outside to weep together. Wallace sat motionless, gazing at his deceased child.

"Mother, she wanted to be buried on the Island. She said those were her happiest days. There is a spot at the top of the hill overlooking the sea. It was our favorite place. We spent a lot of time there talking and laughing and planning our life. I want to bury her there," Patrick said.

"We will leave for there in the morning," Molly said.

"You don't need to go. You have done enough for us," Patrick said.

"I loved her like she was my own. Of course, I will go. We will take her father as well. He should be there."

The men Danny had sent to see about Mickey returned with news that he had been arrested but would likely be released soon. Danny wanted to go immediately, but after thinking about it and remembering what he'd promised his mother, he decided it was best he stay with his sisters. He sent several men to Belfast to do what they could.

It was a long sad ride to the Island. Lucy's casket was in the back of the wagon. There was little talking along the way. Everything had already been said. Lucy was gone. So were Patrick's dreams. Wallace was also devastated and filled with regret. He could have been a better father. He should have spent more time with her. He traded all that for whiskey. It was a bad bargain he wished that he could take back. Molly was also depressed. There were too many losses for her to handle, first Finnegan then Sean and Michael, and now this. She was losing everyone she loved, one at a time.

"What will we do with Wallace?" Patrick asked one evening when he and Molly were alone.

"He is Lucy's father. He is family now," Molly said.

"It's not going to be the easy life he is used to."

"We can't help that. And we can't just leave him."

"You are right. Lucy loved him. I don't understand how she could, but she did, so I'll have to learn to love him too. For Lucy," he said.

The cell where Mickey was being held was a big room filled with about forty or fifty men. Men came and went as they were processed, so it was not possible to keep an accurate count. Being processed meant that the police interviewed you a few times and then decided if you should be released or go before the magistrate. Mickey had been there for two days.

Mickey told them he was Leo Carville. It was a safe name. Leo was an old man who lived in the hills and didn't get involved in anything. Mickey was thinking that might have been a better life for him. It had been hard burying his two boys. It was all his fault. If he had not been so active in the resistance, they both would be alive today. A few of the men in his cell knew who he was, but they would not talk. He was Leo to them.

When they brought him before the police captain for his final interview before being released or charged, he told them his story. He was nowhere near the riot. Which was true. They decided he was not involved so he was released with only a fine. His fine just happened to be the exact amount of money he had in his pocket when they picked him up. Mickey didn't care. He wanted to get back to his family. They needed to get out of Ireland. He should have never come to Belfast.

As he was being escorted out a man on the street recognized him and shouted his name. Mickey kept his head down. The man shouted again using his full name.

"Mickey Delaney is that you?" the man insisted.

The policeman took hold of him again and marched him back to the captain. They were all familiar with the name Mickey Delaney.

The police captain was thrilled. He had Mickey placed in a small cell away from the others. He dispatched a courier to London to inform Peel that they had their man. They would beat the truth out of him and all the Delaneys would soon be apprehended.

Unaware of Mickey's plight, Molly, Patrick, and Wallace finally reached the Island. It was as beautiful as they remembered. They had the service as soon as they could. It was a small gathering—Patrick, Molly, Wallace, and the family who looked after the cottage. Lucy had been fond of them. They had hired a few men to dig the grave. The men also built a large cross that they mounted near the grave. It was the highest spot on the island and the cross could be seen for miles. Patrick was pleased with that. He thought Lucy would approve. The grave was not easy to dig because the ground was mostly rock, but they completed it and the service took place late in the evening so they could see the sunset over the water together one last time.

The service was not the usual memorial. Molly read from Psalms:

"Thou hast set our iniquities before thee, our secret sins in the light of thou countenance. For all our days are passed away in thy wrath; we spend our years as a tale to be told. The days of our years are threescore years and ten: and if by reason of strength, they be fourscore years, yet is their strength labor and sorrow; for it is soon cut off, and we fly away. Who knoweth the power of thy anger, so is thy wrath? So, teach us to number our days, that we may apply our hearts unto wisdom. Return, O Lord, how long? And let it repent thee concerning thy servants. O satisfy us early with thy mercy; that we may rejoice and be glad all our days."

After the reading everyone crossed themselves and Patrick dropped a handful of dirt on the casket. Then they looked at Wallace and he told a few stories about Lucinda when she was small. The most notable one had to do with her imaginary friend. Her friend was a fairy princess named Madge. Madge had a magic wand and would wave it at adults when they argued. This magic made them stop arguing and suddenly get along. Wallace was a good storyteller, and they appreciated knowing these things from Lucy's childhood.

The last thing they did before sunset was listen to Patrick sing to Lucy once more. She loved his voice and they had sat together for hours with him singing to her. Her favorite was "Kilkelly".

Kilkelly, Ireland, 18 and 50 my loving son John
Your good friend the schoolmaster Pat McNamara's so good
As to write these words down
Your brothers have all gone to find work in England
The house is so empty and sad
The crops of potatoes is sorely infected,
A third to half of the bad.
And your sister Brigid and Patrick O'Donnell
Are to be married in June.
Your mother says not to work on the railroad
And be sure to come home soon.
Kilkelly, Ireland this mother is missing her loving son John
Hello to your Mrs. and to your four children,
May they grow healthy and strong.
Michael has got in a wee bit of trouble,
I guess that he never will learn.
Because of the dampness there is no turf to speak of
And now we have nothing to burn.
And Brigid is happy, you named a child for her
And now she has six of her own
You say you have work, but done say
What kind or when you will be coming home.

He sang until it was dark, then they left the men to cover the grave by lantern light. The next morning, they left the island.

Mickey stood silent before the magistrate and the police captain. When he refused to talk, he was escorted by three policemen to a room off the court. It was then he realized that he was not going to get out of this. They planned to do to him what they did to Sean. He was not going to allow them that pleasure. He would make his stand here and take out as many of them as he could. Today was his last day. He smiled at the guards.

"So, Delaney are you going to tell me where your boys are?" the largest of the policemen said.

The three policemen and Mickey were alone in the same small room. They had spent most of the day before questioning him. The questioning only stopped when Mickey was unconscious. Mickey was bruised badly from the beatings.

"You have already killed my boys," Mickey said with hatred.

"Ah, you can talk. I know there are more of them."

Mickey had not said a word since. The last few days had been a continuous pattern of them asking him questions, followed by silence, then a beating. Each night when he got back to his cell, he was barely alive. He was not going to go through this anymore. He was chained at his ankles and his wrists. He was ready for this to end.

"We know you know where they are," the guard continued.

"You Tans are too stupid to know anything," Mickey said.

The man started towards Mickey. Mickey jumped up and head-butted him solidly. The crown of Mickey's head landed squarely in the man's face. Blood gushed from his mouth and nose. He went down, but not before Mickey wrapped the chains around his neck. As he fell Mickey jerked up breaking his neck. Everyone in the room heard it snap.

The other two men rushed at Mickey. They grabbed him as he tried to free his chains from the dead man. He landed an elbow in the stomach of the man on his left, wheeled around, and swung the chains at the other man. The man ducked and only received a glancing blow. The man he'd elbowed recovered quickly and pulled out a club. Mickey then charged the first man and tackled him. He was trying to get the chains around his neck when everything went black. The man with the club had landed a death blow to the top of the Irishman's head. Mickey would never fight again.

That afternoon, a letter from Peel arrived instructing the captain to make sure nothing happened to Delaney before his arrival. It was too late. They would get no information from Mickey Delaney.

CHAPTER 18

Leaving Ireland

The trip from the Island to the coastal cottage where the family waited was uneventful, but it was the worst trip Molly had ever made. She had buried her daughter-in-law and her first grandchild, not even knowing if it was a girl or a boy. She was watching her beloved son in total agony and there was nothing she could do about it. She was losing her loved ones at an alarming rate and she could do nothing about that, either. For years the family had seemed to beat the odds. Her husband and sons were in a dangerous business but they had always returned alive. Now their luck was running out and fate was demanding too high a toll.

Patrick was sinking into a deep depression. He and Lucy had cherished such high hopes. Now he had nothing. His mind would not allow him to do anything except grieve his wife. He knew he should be comforting his mother but he had no energy left for anything but sorrow. He had looked forward to being a father. He knew Lucy would be a loving mother. Now his wife and child were in the cold, rocky ground on an Island in Northern Ireland. He could not bear it. He wanted the hurting to stop, but it would not. Sleep never came and he had eaten nothing for days.

Wallace wasn't any better. He had nothing left to live for. His inheritance, his position, his wife, his daughter, his grandchild—all were gone, never to return. He had always used the bottle as an escape. Now he had no whiskey and the odd thing was that he didn't want it. He could not escape from his sorrow. He deserved what he was getting. He hoped he wouldn't live too long. He was too much a coward to end it.

Several of Mickey's men escorted them, keeping them moving in the right direction. They had no idea what to say or how they could help so they stayed quiet and tended to the grieving party.

At the cottage on the coast, Barney McCormick had just arrived. He wanted to be there before Molly returned. Mickey's faithful friend was becoming the family's champion. The purpose of his trip was to tell Molly in person what had happened to Mickey. News of his death had made its way to almost every village in Ireland. He wanted to be there when she learned the truth.

Before Mickey was arrested, he and Barney had talked about getting the family out of Ireland. Since Mickey was gone now, Barney took it upon himself to facilitate their departure. Mickey's death had complicated matters, however. Peel's men had a new and fervent desire to find the remaining Delaneys. It would be a challenge getting them together and booking passage out of Ireland without the authorities getting wind of it. The bigger problem was Molly. Would she even go now with Mickey gone? Barney had to do his best for his old friend.

Barney had arranged for Mickey's body to be transported to Galway for burial. The British did not want to release the body to him. They wanted a family member to take possession so they could arrest another Delaney. Because of Barney's position and his wealth, he was ultimately able to get the body, though it cost him dearly.

The official cause of death was recorded as natural causes. No one believed that version of things.

Barney had already arranged passage for Patrick and Danny on one of his ships carrying hardware to Boston. Papers had been created with new identities for the brothers and instructions for Roger O'Toole, the owner of the O'Toole Furniture Company there. Roger was also Molly's cousin. Barney had learned that the British did not have John Delaney listed as a target, so his immediate concern was for Patrick and Danny.

John and the girls would stay with Barney until Molly returned from Galway. Arrangements would be made for Molly to visit Mickey's grave secretly before she and the others left on different ships. Their destination had not yet been decided.

They went into the cottage together—Patrick, Danny, Molly, John, and Barney.

"Mickey is dead," Barney said.

It was all he could manage. Molly's face bore a look of disbelief and her body went limp. She had nothing left. John caught her before she hit the floor.

Patrick swallowed hard, then walked out of the cottage and down to the water. He sat by himself in the sand, watching the waves roll in until long after dark. Danny and John managed to get their mother as comfortable as possible. They held her hands long into the night.

"John, it's not right," Barney said. "No boy your age should be given this task, but we have no other choice. It will have to be you caring for your mother and your sisters through this."

Barney told John what he had to do. He told him about the arrangements for Danny and Patrick, and he was going over what John had to do to get his mother to Galway safely when Molly opened her eyes. She had been conscious for a few minutes and was listening to Barney.

"Mrs. Delaney, I am so sorry it has to be like this," Barney said. "Mickey had me take an oath, and I will go to my grave honoring my dear friend's requests."

Molly took his hand.

"I have loved my dear Ireland all my life, but I am not sad to leave her," she said, "The sorrow visited upon this family is more than I can bear. I buried two sons who were killed for no reason. Then I had to watch my sweet Patrick bury his wife and unborn baby. Now the love of my life has been murdered. Barney, I am ready to leave. I will not put up a fight. All the fight has left me. All I have now are the children the British haven't murdered yet."

"Mrs. Delaney, we will do whatever we can to make things better for you. I know your losses are incalculable."

"There is one more thing you can do for me," she said.

She paused, then spoke with purpose.

"I'd like for us to have a celebration. It is what we Irish do, you know. We never did properly celebrate Michael's, Sean's, and Lucy's lives. I think this family needs a good celebration before we go our separate ways. I want them to remember the good things about their brothers and father. Can you arrange this?"

"We Scots are much like our Irish brethren, we too love a good wake," Barney agreed.

"I want as many of Michael's men as we can gather to be here. They loved him as we did," Molly added, "And though I know I'm asking too much, there is one more thing you must do for us," Molly said.

"Anything, dear lady."

"Wallace Conway is Lucy's father. Can you arrange passage for him with Patrick? Patrick will be caring for him. He is family now, too."

"Consider it done," he said, as he patted her hand.

Word got around about the wake. Everyone close enough to make it came, partly because they wanted to honor Mickey and his boys and partly because they would not miss a good wake. Barney had hired musicians so there was plenty of dancing. He provided the food, and the alcohol was plentiful. Everyone enjoyed the whiskey except Wallace. He had promised Lucy he would never take another drink. It was difficult, but he planned to keep that promise.

Molly insisted there would be no tears and no sadness this day. It was a day for them to remember the good things about her husband and sons. Toasts and stories were plentiful and the laughter was intoxicating. Even Patrick ate something as he enjoyed the good memories with his loved ones. This was exactly how Molly wanted to remember her native land. A land filled with laughter, joy, and family.

The party went on late into the night and most of the guests ended up staying until daybreak. They sang and drank into the night over a bonfire on the beach. Elizabeth fell asleep in Nelly's lap. It was a day they would all remember.

The following afternoon Molly, John, and the girls left for Galway. They were escorted by a band of Mickey's men. Danny, Patrick, and Wallace were taken to the ship that would bear them to their new home in America.

McCormick, Patrick, and Danny sat on a bench on the bridge, watching the cargo as it was loaded. The ship was named the Matilda. She was a cargo ship and her cargo on this trip was people—poor people with one-way tickets to Boston. The lower cargo hull hold had been converted into sleeping quarters. On the return trip, the same room would be full of tobacco. Men, women, and children were crowded together.

Wallace had remained sober since Lucy's death. He had made her a promise he intended to keep. He was a broken man—sad, lonely, and full of guilt. He occupied his time reading novels. He would bury himself in the pages to escape his pain. Sometimes it worked for a few hours. Then his pain returned. He was haunted by his own story, one sadder than any he could read.

"Patrick, you know that you are turning into Wallace, don't you?" Danny asked.

Patrick frowned.

"Do you want me to get one of his cheap novels for you to read?"

"You talk too much," Patrick replied.

"The way I see it is this. You are at some kind of crossroads and you can't choose which way is best. One way is that you can choose to deal with your loss and move on. Like we all have done. The way we were taught. Or you can cling to your grief and become Wallace."

Patrick fixed his eyes on a distant spot, far out in the water. He was trying to ignore his brother.

"I want to know what I am to call you," Danny said.

Patrick remained silent.

"Is it Paddy, or should I call you Little Wally?"

"Will you shut up?" Patrick asked.

"So, I guess it's Little Wally."

"Will you let it go?" Patrick begged.

"No, I won't. I have lost my father and two brothers. I don't know when or if I'll see Mam, John, and the girls again. I don't want to lose you too. So quit being such a baby and get over it. We all are having to do that. You can too. For God's sake, you are a Delaney."

Danny let out a long audible breath and got up to walk away.

"Where are you going?" Patrick asked.

"To get one of Wallace's novels," he replied.

"You've made your point. Now come back here and sit down. We need to evaluate the passengers. Some of them may be worth dealing with. We will probably need a few good men when we get to Boston. It can't hurt to form some alliances before we arrive," Patrick said.

"I may have it all wrong. You may be turning into Michael," said his brother.

By the time they reached Boston, the Delaney boys had their crew. They had selected four men and had befriended them and their families. They arrived in Boston and went to work for their kinsman. Roger O'Toole was an ornery old man and hard to work for, but he was fair.

Several months after they arrived, Wallace died. There had been no warning signs. He had been reading a Walter Scott novel.

Back in Galway, the last of the Delaney clan had arrived at the gravesite. Barney McCormick had placed stone monuments on the graves of Mickey and his boys. Mickey's was inscribed with the following words:

Here lies Michael Delaney
a True Hero of his People
and a National Treasure of Ireland

Molly spent half the day there. She spoke audibly to her sons and her husband as if they could hear her. She told them about Lucy's death and the service they held for her on the hill. She told them all about how Patrick had taken Wallace in and cared for him. She told them about the wake and what each man had said as he toasted their beloved Mickey and his boys. She cried openly as she shared her heart with them about how afraid she was to go on without them. All the while, John stood silently at his mother's side.

"Maybe I'm crazy talking to Mickey and the boys, John. Your father and I talked about everything, all the time, our whole lives. It can't just be over now..."

John fought back his own tears as his mother continued the one-way conversations.

She told them about how Patrick and Danny were on their way to Boston to work for the O'Toole. She told them that she and the others would leave soon. She had no idea where they would go. She asked Mickey what he thought as she went down her list of places they might go. Somehow it felt right to her. If she was crazy, it would just be one more thing she had to endure. She thought she could hear Mickey's voice — *You must get through this. You can do it.*

When she could cry no more, she gathered her remaining children and walked away. She never looked back.

C H A P T E R 19

New World

Five months after Patrick, Danny, and Wallace arrived in Boston, the rest of the Delaneys were just beginning their voyage to America. Molly had received two letters from Boston, the first from Danny telling them that they were well. They were settling in and Boston was filled with Irishmen, so it was beginning to feel like home. The second letter was from Patrick, telling her Wallace had died. Hearing from the boys cheered Molly up. There was something else that brought a measure of joy to her again during this period. She had made friends with Catherine Clancy, a lady's maid in McCormick's house. She and Molly had much in common as Catherine had lost her husband recently and her only son had been killed working on the railroad. When Barney McCormick realized how close they had become, he decided it would be good for them both to start a new life in New York.

The day finally arrived when the Delaneys and Catherine were to leave. Unlike the ship Patrick and Danny had taken, this was a true cargo ship. It was owned by McCormick. The captain was a Scotsman named Spencer; the first mate was a retired British sailor named Edwin Parker. Parker was made to relinquish his cabin, which was next to the captain's quarters, for Molly, Catherine, and the girls. John was to bunk with the sailors, which was where Parker would also have to sleep. The

143

man was furious. He couldn't complain because McCormick owned the ship, but he made no bones about his bitterness in Spencer's absence. John had his first encounter with Parker the day they boarded the ship. John had helped his mother and sisters get settled into their room then he went below to find his bunk. There were two empty bunks, both identical. John selected the first one he saw and put his things on that bunk. Then he went up on the deck to look around. After the ship pulled away, John took the girls to their cabin and checked on his mother. She just didn't want to see them leave. He went below and saw all his belongings piled up in a corner. Parker was stretched out on the bunk that John had chosen.

"I like this spot better," Parker said.

"You could have just asked," John said.

Parker sat up and gave him a hard stare through hateful eyes. He stood up. He was a tall, muscular man with several inches on John.

"I'll not be asking you anything. I'll be telling you what it will be. I should be in my cabin but I'm here because of you people. So, if I were you, I should not cross me again. Keep your mouth shut and stay out of my way. I know who you are," Parker said.

John held his temper and quietly put his kit on the vacant bunk. John was not afraid of him—maybe he should have been, but he wasn't. John left the room and found Nelly.

"Nelly, you have always done such a wonderful job of caring for your sister. Mam can barely care for herself now since Paw is gone so I need you to do all you can to take care of Elizabeth. Catherine will help you, but I know you will take good care of her."

"Why do we have to go through this?" she asked.

"I will never know that. But we must. It is just us now. We must be the family. Mam needs us. She could not make it without the family. And we are it now. Just us."

"It's not right," she said.

"No, it's not. But it is what we have. Father always taught us to deal with what we have, not what we want," John said.

John held Nelly tight, watching Elizabeth play on the deck as Ireland grew smaller in the distance.

The voyage to America took two weeks. The first few days both girls were seasick, so it was not pleasant. They eventually got used to the pitch of the ship and learned to enjoy it. Little Elizabeth spent most of her days playing on the deck and following the sailors around, asking endless questions about the ship. She was enjoying the adventure. While Nellie busied herself caring for her mother and sister. John spent most of his time pondering what the new world would be like. He loved being with the men, all but Parker. John made a point to steer clear of him.

From the beginning, he never saw Molly without Catherine. The two women had been close when they left Ireland, but now they were inseparable. After a few days, Molly was beginning to perk up and she spent more time with the girls talking to them about their lessons, but Catherine was right there too. Molly told them about how she thought life would be in America. She told them about strange new places they would see. John thought maybe she was turning the corner and accepting their plight.

John was with some sailors one day when Parker walked up on them.

"Stop wasting your time with that boy," Parker said.

"Aye aye," the sailor answered.

"You lazy, good-for-nothing slug," Parker said to John.

He blew his whistle and when all the men around stopped to hear what he was about to say, he spoke in a loud voice.

"Men, you will no longer spend any time with this sorry creature here." He was pointing at John. "His name is Delazy and he is worthless. Don't let me catch you with him again."

John stood up and took a couple of steps toward Parker. He was held back by a couple of sailors.

"Now what is it you were about to do Delazy?" Parker asked, grinning.

He knew the label he'd put on John irritated him. From that day forward all he ever called him was Delazy. And he was correct. It did irritate John. His hatred for Parker was mounting.

It was in the early morning on the sixth day of their journey that it all changed again. The women were in their cabin and Nelly and Elizabeth were playing on the deck.

John ruffled Elizabeth's hair.

"You be careful, little sailor girl," he said, grinning at his baby sister.

Nelly pulled her away from John, scolding him playfully.

"Go on about your work, John. She's my responsibility!"

Just then, there was a snapping sound, high above the deck. As a pulley worked loose from the top of the main mast, something caught Elizabeth's eye and she turned.

John turned at the same moment and he saw the pulley fall. He raced to Elizabeth but was too late.

The blow crushed her skull and she died instantly. Nelly and John, frozen in place, looked down in horror at the motionless body of their little sister—gone from life to death in only an instant.

Molly and Catherine ran out of the cabin when they heard Nelly scream. John had gathered the little girl up in his arms. Molly fell on John and her baby, crying bitterly. Catherine was shocked but she knew enough to get Molly away from the child. She wrestled her back into the cabin.

A crowd had gathered. Nelly was shaking violently. John laid Elizabeth down gently and took Nelly in his arms. He was covered with the blood of his dead sister. Nelly went limp and for a moment John feared that she, too, was dead. Several different seamen gave reports of the accident when the captain arrived. Everyone seemed to be talking at once, but through the maze of voices, John heard one voice over all the others. It was Parker.

"No great loss. Just one less useless Irish brat. That one was always underfoot. Good riddance," he said.

Several sailors restrained John, as others gently wrapped little Elizabeth in clean sailcloth.

"Go be with your mother, son," said the captain. "There is nothing else you can do for this wee child."

John took Nelly back to the cabin where Catherine was tending to Molly. He stayed there with his family. It was the hardest thing he had ever done. He wanted to seek out Parker and beat him senseless. The rage inside him was building by the minute as he watched his mother and sister tormented. After a while, Nelly was asleep in Molly's arms and Molly was staring into space with a distant look in her eyes. Catherine left Molly for a brief time to talk with John.

"It was nobody's fault," she whispered to John.

"Nelly blames herself, but you are right, it was not her fault," John said.

"Nelly will be all right eventually. I am not talking about Nelly. I'm talking about you," Catherine said.

She sat beside him and held his hand. John did not like to be touched so he pulled away. She took his hand again more firmly.

"I can see you are angry and have assigned that blame to someone. That is foolish. It is nobody's fault. I know that man Parker has been bothering you. Regardless of what he said, it is not his fault. Sometimes these things happen. His harsh words didn't do this. They were mean, but he didn't kill Elizabeth. I don't want you to leave here until you realize this," Catherine said.

John knew she was right. But he still hated Parker.

The family was devastated anew. Molly withdrew from everyone, even Catherine. Nelly took it hardest because she blamed herself. It was her responsibility to care for her sister. She had failed. John was sad too. He loved his sister so he would not allow himself to fall apart. It was his responsibility now to ensure that they got past this. He took it upon himself to take control. There was nobody else. He forced his feelings away, pushing them down deep inside. For now, he must be the rock. He must be strong for his mother and sister. It is what his father would expect.

They buried the child at sea the next day. John and Catherine watched her float away on the little raft the sailors had made. Neither Nelly nor his mother could bear to be there. The rest of the voyage passed in grief and sadness.

Life on the ship was miserable now for Nelly. Everything she saw reminded her of the trauma of her baby sister's head being crushed beneath the falling iron.

"The sailors tell me we are close to land," John told her as they sat one day, looking out on the open water.

"How do they know that? It all looks the same to me," Nelly asked.

"I guess they know how long it takes, plus they have signs they can read, like more seabirds or the winds. I don't really know, but I'm ready to be on solid land again."

"Do you think we will ever be happy?"

"Nelly I will do everything I can to make sure we are happy again. You can count on that," John said.

Two days after that conversation, they spotted land. It was a long way out, but it was there. This gave John a little hope. Molly sensed his hope, and she hugged her two children.

"We will get through this. Your father is depending on us."

That was all she could say. John hoped it was true. He was having his doubts. It seemed like nothing would ever be right again with the

Delaneys. He kept these thoughts to himself and forced a smile for Nelly's benefit.

Their troubles were far from over. Life in New York would be hard, though less so than for earlier Irish migrants.

In 1847, at the height of the potato famine, there had been an estimated 350,000 European immigrants to the new world. The largest group was the Irish. At the time, there was no national strategy to handle the aliens. Each local city took in as many as they thought they could handle, then sent the rest to find other places to live. That year New York accepted an estimated 145,890 people while Boston took another 6,670 new citizens. Philadelphia received over 13,000 and New Orleans took 40,442. Many others were turned away to find homes in either Quebec, New Brunswick, or other Canadian cities.

Many were in poor health. Typhus was common. It was known as "ship fever." Of all the immigrants, the Irish were in the worst conditions. They would normally land at Grosse Isle. The locals referred to it as the 'Isle of Death.' Typhus was contracted by body lice. Within ten days of being bitten, the person would experience symptoms of high fever, muscle pain, and severe headaches. If the patient lived three days they would usually recover, however, typhus would often recur years later, causing death in most cases.

Now, as the Delaneys were arriving in America, New York had a more organized method of dealing with newcomers. They were held in quarantine for fourteen days. During this time, local businessmen looking for laborers would show up and hire whomever they found to meet their needs. If they didn't get hired during that period, the immigrants were released and encouraged to find another city. There were no funds for this, so rather than leave the city, the immigrants usually wandered the streets of New York until they found employment.

The Delaneys' troubles continued the day they got off the ship. As they were disembarking, John saw Parker talking to an official. He was pointing at them. The man came towards them with Parker following. Then the man explained to them that they would need to be taken to the quarantine area for processing. Since it wasn't a passenger ship, they had hoped to avoid that process. But Parker was intent on causing them problems. John saw the first mate grinning. He knew how horrible the quarantine facilities were. As the man led the four of them toward an office, John told the official he'd forgotten something on the ship and needed to go back. The man agreed, and John ran back to the ship. As soon as he boarded the ship, he saw Parker.

"Why did you tell them about us? It is a cargo ship. They never would have looked for us," John asked.

"Because I wanted to," Parker replied.

"We never did anything to you," John said.

"You took my cabin," Parker said.

"The women couldn't bunk with these men. It was all that the captain could do. I did as you asked, and I stayed out of your way the entire trip. And now you did this," John said.

"Yes, I did. And I would do it again, Delazy," Parker said.

John lunged at him, throwing a punch that landed square on his chin. He put all his weight and strength into that punch. There was a crunching sound—the sound of bones cracking. Parker's head snapped backward, and he went down hard. John stood over him. Parker's eyes rolled back in his head. He was out cold. His body stiffened up and he quivered a few times. The sailors watched frozen in place. John stepped away and turned to leave.

"Bravo, mate," a sailor said.

"He had it coming," another one added.

Then one of them started clapping. As John left the ship, he heard them cheering him. He didn't look back. He needed to get away from there as soon as he could. He looked down at his right hand. It was already swelling. The crack was not only Parker's jaw. Several small bones in John's hand were also broken.

By the time he reached the office, the women had been processed and were waiting to be transported to the quarantine station. Molly looked down at his swollen hand. She knew what had happened. John started to make up a story to tell her. As soon as he opened his mouth she spoke.

"Please don't lie to me, John. I can't take it if my youngest son lies to me."

They would never again speak of what happened that day. John knew that it was some kind of omen—that violence was sure to follow him wherever he went.

C H A P T E R 20

America

The immigrant quarantine shelter at the port of New York was nothing more than an old warehouse filled with cots, and Molly and Catherine began to care for the sick immediately upon their arrival. Many had typhoid and the place smelled of filth and death. Molly came down with a fever within days of their arrival and was gravely ill for three days, and while Nelly and Catherine never left her side, John could not stop pacing. On the fourth day, she began to improve. She recovered, but the fever left her weak and frail.

Two days before they were to be released, a well-dressed man showed up with a package from Barney McCormick.

"Mr. McCormick has paved the way for you, my friends. I am Silas Crowe, at your service."

He patted John on the back as he introduced himself, tipping his hat to the ladies.

"Mrs. Clancy? he asked, looking first at Molly and then at Catherine.

Catherine hesitated, then stepped forward.

Before she could speak, he handed her a letter.

"Is this about…" she started, then broke off as he interrupted her question,

"It's from a wealthy gentleman who does a lot of business with McCormick," he said. "It guarantees you a position as lady's maid for his wife."

Catherine closed her eyes and raised the letter briefly to her lips.

"I'm so sorry," she said, suddenly embarrassed. "I had hoped, but I didn't know…"

"They are expecting your arrival in two days, ma'am," he said. "You'll find the address and everything else you need to know in this letter."

Catherine hugged Molly, a hint of a tear in her eye.

For the first time since Elizabeth's death, Nelly brightened.

"Do you have a letter for us, too?"

"Let's see," he said, "Why yes, I have something for a Mrs. Molly Delaney. Would that be you, young lady?"

Nelly giggled.

"No! I'm Nelly! Mrs. Delaney is my mam!"

Molly gave a demure curtsy.

"May I have the letter please, Mr. Crowe?"

"It is more than just a letter, Mrs. Delaney. But first, let me say that it is an honor to meet you and your family. Even here we have heard of the brave deeds of Mickey Delaney and his sons."

"We thank you," she said, "and we are grateful for your help. It has been a difficult journey since leaving Ireland and yours is the first friendly face we've seen."

From his leather valise, Crowe extracted several documents.

"First, there is the matter of your place of residence. Perhaps we will be able to improve upon your situation eventually, but for now, you will lodge above a tavern. However, the room is clean and well-ventilated, and there are simple but adequate furnishings."

He had dreaded this particular speech, wondering how the storied Delaney family would react to such modest accommodations. Molly was quick to answer.

"Mr. Crowe, we have just spent the last six weeks first in the hold of a terrible ship filled with sick, desperate people and then in this dreadful shelter. We have sacrificed privacy and comfort and we have lost…"

Her voice trailed off before the sadness over Elizabeth's cruel death could spill over into her words.

Catherine whispered to Crowe as Molly fell silent.

"Oh, my dear Mrs. Delaney, I am so sorry for your tragic loss, so very sorry indeed. And I regret that your lodgings are not more appropriate…"

"No, please do not misunderstand me," she said, collecting herself. "It has been a difficult journey and we are tired and grieving still, but I can assure you we are not discouraged at the prospect of living in clean, well-ventilated lodgings, even if they are atop a saloon."

John's gaze was fixed on the man, but he threw a sidelong glance at his mother. Where did her strength come from? What kind of woman could endure the hell she had been through and still remain so poised—even grateful?

Crowe sighed with relief.

"Here you are, then, Mrs. Delaney. This receipt will prove that Mr. McCormick has paid three months' rent in advance on your room."

Now it was Molly with tears in her eyes.

"Be sure to keep this paper, safe, madam," he added. "I've met your rent collector and he is not exactly a gentleman. In fact, he is a rascal. He may try to cheat you, but as long as you have this receipt, there's little he can do."

"How will we ever repay Barney's kindness?" she said. looking from John to Nelly.

Crowe cleared his throat, moved by her gratitude.

"There is also this," he said, handing her a card with something written on it.

"What is it?" Nelly begged, unable to wait for her mother.

"Well now, miss, this is the address of one of the finest leather shops in all the city," said Crowe. "Your sainted mother need only call on the proprietor, Ephraim Quigley, to secure highly advantageous work as a skilled assistant to one of the leather workers in his employ. He is aware that she has only just arrived from abroad and will require some time to become settled before commencing work."

Nelly giggled.

John, standing behind Crowe, had begun to imitate the man with exaggerated gestures, silently aping his flowery speech.

Molly gave John a pointed look.

"Isn't it kind of Mr. Crowe to have made all these arrangements for us on Barney's behalf, John?" she said, "and he's come all this way just to welcome us, too!"

John hung his head.

"Oh, Mr. Delaney! I almost forgot," Crowe said, turning to John.

"I'm not Mr. Delaney."

John was embarrassed now.

"John, then," said Crowe, "the youngest warrior of the clan, I'm told?"

John nodded uncomfortably.

"Here I have a letter on your behalf for a Mr. Jonathan Lewis. He is a politician with much influence over what goes on at the docklands. Go to his office as soon as you get settled and present this letter of introduction. He will see to it that you get a good job on the right crew."

Molly gave John another pointed look. He stood up straight. Bold in battle and skilled in the strategy of war, John was still painfully insecure in the ordinary business of communicating with others. He took a deep breath.

"Thank you, sir. Not just for this but for everything you have done for us today."

"Quite all right," said Crowe. "Now, I've taken the liberty of bringing a hamper of provisions for the family. Word is the food in quarantine is none too good, and you'll all need your strength, what with new jobs and challenges ahead."

Nelly could restrain herself no longer. She was overwhelmed by the unexpected kindness of their benefactor. Impulsively, she threw her arms around his neck, then just as quickly, she pulled back, mortified by her own forwardness.

"Oh, please forgive me," she said. "It's just that you are so kind, and we are so hungry, and you have brought us food… and hope!"

Crowe smiled at her.

"Miss Delaney, you are very welcome. I have two daughters of my own, and it is my honor to provide some small comfort to the daughter of a great Irish chieftain," he said, in a gentle voice.

The man turned to Molly and bowed slightly.

"Now, eat and take your rest, Delaney family. Your new life in America is about to begin. I will call for you in two days' time. Good day for now."

On their last morning in quarantine, Molly woke before dawn. She was still weak, but she had eaten a nourishing meal from Crowe's hamper the evening before and she was beginning to feel like herself again. Pale, gray light sifted through the high windows in the former warehouse. The early morning sounds were those to which she had become accustomed since leaving Ireland: a cacophony of coughing, moaning, and snoring, punctuated by the raucous screech of seabirds.

"Mam?"

Nelly had slipped out of her cot and was standing at her mother's elbow.

"Shhhh. Don't wake your brother."

"A bit late for that," John muttered.

"We will say goodbye to Catherine today," Molly whispered. "I will miss my friend…"

"But we won't miss this bloody hellhole," John interjected.

"Mind your tongue, John."

He was the man of the family now, and yet in so many ways, he was still a boy. The burden of being John's only surviving parent weighed heavily on Molly.

By noon, Silas Crowe had returned, and as soon as they were processed and released from quarantine, his men loaded their meager belongings onto the back of a wagon carrying kegs of ale. Silas and Catherine then bade them farewell, and an hour later, after having been bumped and jolted over the rough, cobblestone streets of New York, they stopped in front of what Molly assessed as a less-than-respectable drinking establishment. She was an Irishwoman though, and the mother of many sons, so she was not deterred by either the sights or the sounds. As they climbed the stairs to their shabby lodgings above the saloon, John avoided his mother's gaze.

Inside their room, he looked around, sick at heart over their pending prospects.

"It's not much, Mam…"

Even with the door closed, they could hear the clatter and low roar of conversation from downstairs.

"It is home for now," Molly replied.

Her mouth was set. She allowed no expression to betray the merest hint of dismay as she unpacked their belongings.

Nelly looked at first her mother, then John, as she set the family prayer book on the bedside table.

"We can make this a fine home…" she said, unconvinced.

John's hand was beginning to heal and the swelling was almost gone. He was resolved to go to Mr. Lewis as soon as possible to secure work on the docks. For now, he struggled for something to say that might make things better in this room, but he came up empty.

Molly said it instead.

"This is not the first time we Delaneys have faced hard times. We are sad, yes, and our situation is uncomfortable. We have lost much—more than most—but we are still here," she said.

Her eyes brimmed with tears but her voice was strong and unwavering.

"And we have each other. Tonight, I am thinking of the courageous husband and sons I have lost—your father and brothers—and I am taking strength from their sacrifice. Now I expect you to do the same. Feeling sorry for ourselves will never improve our lot."

That night they slept soundly. The New York street noises and the clatter from the saloon sang a lullaby to their exhausted hearts. The Delaney blood coursing through their veins warmed them, and their proud heritage became a fortress against the rest of the world, at least for the night.

John left early to look for Mr. Lewis, introduction in hand. A few hours later, Molly was making tea on a small alcohol burner when she heard heavy footsteps on the stairs. The door shivered in its frame with the force of a single, thunderous knock. Before she could answer, a heavyset man barged in without permission. He wore a suit but his manners were not those of a gentleman. He scowled, then spit on the floor.

"Jonas Blackman is my name. I'll be collecting rent on the first of each month. If you're late you'll be thrown out by the end of that day," he announced.

"Well, I am pleased to meet you, Mr. Blackman. You may be assured we will not be late with the rent," Molly said.

She was determined to show no fear.

"I understand you have paid for the first two months," he said.

"You are mistaken sir. We are paid up for three months."

She held out the receipt McCormick had enclosed with his letter. Blackman was caught in a lie, so he waved away the receipt as unworthy of his attention.

"There doesn't seem to be anything here worth much," he said, changing the subject.

His gaze lingered a moment too long on Nelly.

"If you're late on your rent, you'll be out on the street and I'll own everything," he said with finality.

He left as quickly as he had entered, slamming the door behind him.

Nelly was pale with fear.

"He's a bully. We've dealt with them before," Molly said quickly.

Nelly looked at the door.

"He scares me," she whispered.

Molly took Nelly by the shoulders and shook the girl gently.

"No," she said. "We do not have the luxury of fear, my girl. Now drink your tea and read from your prayer book. We will attend mass on Sunday and I need you to reflect on matters of the soul."

Nelly was not comforted and Molly understood why, but she wasn't sure what to do about it. She walked to the window with her tea and surveyed the neighborhood, at least what she could see from her vantage point. It was a far cry from Sunrise Estates, but she was beyond regrets now. She needed to solve the problem of how to keep Nelly safe from Blackman and others of his ilk. It was suddenly clear the girl could not stay here alone during the day.

"Put your hat and coat on," she said, half an hour later. "We need to take a walk."

Lucy was full of questions but knew better than to pester her mother when Molly had that determined look.

A few blocks from the saloon, they found the factory where Molly would be working. She pulled out the card Crowe had given her. They were to look for a Mr. Quigley. Satisfied that she had the right place, Molly gave the door a sharp rap.

"Come in. It's not locked," a male voice answered.

Inside, as their eyes adjusted to the dim lighting, they saw him, a thin, seemingly nervous man with wire-rim glasses. His coarse, curly hair was ungroomed and sticking out in all directions. He was standing behind a work table piled with leather.

"Yes, what do you want? I'm Quigley. What brings you here?"

"Mr. Quigley, my name is Molly Delaney. Barney McCormick told me you might have work for me," she said.

He scratched his head, then appeared to remember.

"Ah, yes. Mrs. Delaney. It's a good thing you came today," he said. "I was afraid I might have to give your job away. I really couldn't wait another week."

"I am ready to work," she said, "but I have a problem…"

Quigley launched into a paroxysm of coughing. He pulled out his handkerchief and mopped his face, peering at them through thick lenses.

"I don't need any problems," he said, his voice matter of fact. "I only need workers. And workers with problems is not what I want."

"I will be no problem for you. I am only asking if my daughter may accompany me to work. You will hardly know she's here. I am on my own, you see, and I cannot leave her alone and unprotected while I am here."

He pushed back from his chair and stood up. He was taller than he looked sitting down. He seemed to be all legs, like a giant benevolent spider. He paced the floor behind his desk a few times, took a long look at Nelly, then put his hands on his desk and leaned forward.

"Frankly, If you were anyone else, I'd have already sent you packing. But your benefactor, Mr. McCormick, is important to me. So, here is what I'll do. I will employ the girl as a runner. I have ten cobblers on the second floor and twelve on the third floor, each with an assistant."

He stopped to indulge in another fit of coughing. When he'd recovered, he continued.

"You, Mrs. Delaney, will be a cobbler's assistant as well. A runner would keep all the assistants supplied with the materials they need so they don't waste their time going up and down. This is an idea I have been thinking about for a while. It should increase production."

Nelly had looked up for the first time. She was hanging onto Mr. Quigley's every word.

"The supplies are on the first floor. The girl will be going up and down the stairs all day long. Can she do that?"

"Oh yes sir, I can surely do that!"

Nelly answered instantly before Molly could say a word.

"I will add an extra two bits to your mother's daily wages," Quigley said. "You both start tomorrow at 8 o'clock sharp. Don't be late."

The sun was setting as John returned. His clothes were sweat-stained and he smelled of fish. Nelly was full of questions.

"Well?" she said.

"They found a place for me right away. I'm on Dock #6."

"Do you like the work?" Molly said.

She was used to laconic Delaney men but today she wanted details and John didn't seem disposed to chat about his day.

"It's work," he said, "and it pays."

He closed his eyes and leaned back in his chair, stretching his back, but did not complain. Molly knew the work was hard and she could see the boy was exhausted.

Nelly brought a cup of tea and some of the leftover bread and cheese from Crowe's hamper

"Eat, John," said Molly. "You have to eat."

"We have things to tell you about!" said Nelly.

She was growing impatient with her brother.

John nodded, took a long sip of his tea, and wiped his mouth on his filthy sleeve.

After supper and a full recitation of the day's events from his mother and sister, John picked up his hat and announced he had an errand to run. He had been silent throughout the recounting of their landlord's uninvited visit, betraying nothing of the anger that was now boiling up in his Delaney heart.

First, he walked around the block, on the chance Nelly or Molly might be standing at the upstairs window. He had no desire to share his plans with them, at least for now. As he rounded the back corner at the rear of the tavern, he slipped in through a side door.

As his eyes adjusted to the dim light, he spotted a table full of young men who bore the unmistakable look of the docks.

"May I join you?"

"Pull up a chair, Irish," said one.

"New to the neighborhood, or new to the country?" another asked.

"Both," John replied. "And now, at the docks.'

That prompted a round of stories about the infamous port of New York. A heated discussion of the pros and cons of dock work followed.

John nodded, feigning more interest than he felt. He had spotted the man who matched Nelly's description of their unwelcome visitor at a table across the room.

"See that fellow over there?" he said casually, to the man at his left.

They all looked at once. It was too obvious. John felt foolish. But no one at the man's table had noticed.

"Yea, that's Jonas Blackman," said a red-haired man a little older than John.

"I've seen him around. What's his story?"

"Best to stay away from him," said Red, looking around nervously.

"Is he dangerous?"

"Probably not—he's mostly all talk, I think. But he's in with powerful politicians you don't want to cross."

"Yeah, who would that be?"

"I'd rather not say. I may have said too much already. You don't want to cross these people," Red said quietly.

"Have a drink, so," said one of the older men. "Tell us the news from Ireland."

John grinned and made a few disparaging remarks about the British without revealing his intimate knowledge of the conflict. There was no need to advertise his connection to the great Mickey Delaney. Not here. He and Molly had already decided to leave their stories in Ireland, at least for now. When he left, his pockets were lighter but his surveillance mission had been a success. He would do nothing for now but he would keep Blackman in his sights.

One evening, a few weeks later, John stopped at the tavern again on his way home from work. For some reason, he hated going home now. He hated bringing the stink of the docks into their room, yes, but it was more than that. He had been paying close attention to their dwindling hoard of coins, and he was worried. Every drink he bought was more than they could afford, so he rationed his visits to the bar, but tonight he needed advice. Red and his crew were at the same table. They had already emptied over half a bottle of whiskey and the bar was noisy. When John told Red about his financial troubles, his friend had a solution.

"You'll never make enough working on the docks—no matter how many hours you put in. And you'll ruin your back in the process, " he said.

"What else can I do? I don't have contacts here," John said.

"I know a man."

John sat up straight.

"He's a gambler. But he also does other things. He has money and he pays well."

"Do you work for him?"

"No, I work for my uncle. But if f I didn't have family to lean on, I'd go see him," Red replied.

"Where can I find him?"

"Not in a dive like this."

Red wrote down an address, blew on the paper to dry the ink, then handed it to John. John looked at it, folded it up, and put it in his shirt pocket. He would figure out what it said later. No need to let Red know how ignorant he was.

It took John a couple of days to find someone to read the paper to him. There was a man's name written on it, along with the address of a fancy restaurant with a gaming room in the back. The man was Calvin Stewart.

Molly and Nelly were earning now, and dock work paid well, but John could already see that they would be unable to meet their expenses once the prepaid rent ran out. He knew this was something he couldn't discuss with Molly, but he'd decided he had no choice but to call on this man.

The next day, John left the docks and went straight to the restaurant. At the door, he asked for Mr. Stewart and was told to wait outside. Eventually, he was escorted to an upstairs room. A man was seated at a table in the middle of the room with two beautiful young women. John had seen such women in Galway, but never this close.

"Mr. Stewart, my name is John Delaney, and…"

The man interrupted before he could finish.

"What is this about?"

"I'm looking for work."

Stewart pointed to a desk in the corner. On the desk were a lamp, some papers, and a bottle of Scotch with shot glasses on a silver tray.

"Have a seat, Mr. Delaney," he said. "Now, may I ask, what is it you do? And who told you about me?"

"I was told by a friend. I'd rather not mention his name. And I'll say this: I can do what needs to be done," John said.

Stewart leaned back in his chair.

"I like the fact that you understand discretion and can protect your sources. In other words, I don't like a man that talks too much. It's never good for business. And I may have things that need to be done from time to time."

Stewart put two glasses on the table. He poured the drinks, then handed a glass to John. John touched his glass to Stewart's.

"I guess we have a deal."

"Yes, sir we do," John said.

"I'll get word to you when I need something done," Stewart said. "You know a bar called The Anchor, down by Dock 7?"

John nodded.

The man took a wallet from his breast coat pocket and handed John several banknotes.

"This is payment in advance. See the bartender there on Wednesday after your shift. Tell him your name but don't mention mine. He'll have an envelope for you."

John finished his drink, excused himself, and left the restaurant. When he was outside, he counted the money. It was enough to pay their rent for several months and still have money left over.

Later, it occurred to John that reading the instructions would be an issue. Well, he'd deal with that when it was time. He bought a soup bone and some potatoes and carrots on the way home. They'd had nothing but beans and porridge this week. Tonight's dinner would seem like a feast.

As they enjoyed the evening's repast, Molly and Nelly talked about their work. Molly was good at her job and popular with the other assistants at the leather factory. Nelly, too, had proven herself, scurrying up and down the stairs dozens of times a day, and lightening the load for the artisans. They were both full of stories about their daily experiences, and John was relieved at their chatter. If they were talking, he didn't have to, and the less he talked, the less likely it was that Molly would figure out his secret.

But Molly had secrets of her own. Though she was putting on a brave face for her family, she could not allow herself to be happy again. Guilt had become her constant companion. She had lost almost everything and she harbored an unnatural fear that the little she had left would soon be taken from her as well. She could hardly hold her son or daughter. She thought if she loved them too much they too would die. Worse, she could see and feel the same guilt in Nelly, who had taken her eyes off baby Elizabeth for that fateful instant. Molly took responsibility for it all, and it was crushing her.

The weeks passed, and one Sunday morning, Molly and Nelly were walking to Mass, as was their custom. Neither felt like going after their long work week at the factory. Nelly, sensing her mother was at the breaking point, had encouraged her to talk with a priest. Molly resisted as Nelly insisted. This time, Nelly prevailed.

Before mass, Molly went into the confessional. She began her confession and soon found herself saying more than she had intended to say. She avoided the subject of her despair or her secret thoughts of taking her own life, but after recounting all her losses, the truth came spilling out. She was ashamed and horrified by the darkness in her soul.

After Mass, Molly just wanted to escape. She and Nelly were halfway down the street when a young priest caught up with them. He introduced himself and asked if he could accompany them. You can't tell a priest no, Molly thought. That might be one more sin added to her growing list. She agreed to walk with him. He led them to a café and bought them lunch. Father Matthew, for that was his name, carried the conversation that day since both mother and daughter seemed tongue-tied.

"When I was a boy on the farm my main chore was to milk the cows," he said. "I had to do it so much that I began to hate milk. It was only recently that I learned to like it again. And I am glad I did. I had forgotten how much I loved ice cream. And this café has the best ice cream in the city!"

He waved a waiter over and inquired about the flavors they had that day. After hearing them all Nelly decided on strawberry, Molly wanted chocolate, and Father Matthew selected peach. After lunch, he told them he would look for them again the following Sunday. On the way home, Nelly had a spring in her step.

Over the next few weeks, Father Matthew took them to the same café after Mass each Sunday. Afterward, if the weather was good, they would go for a walk. Somehow, they all became friends. He never questioned Molly about anything or probed in any way. They just talked. They talked about life on the farm where he grew up. Molly would share stories about Ireland. The good memories. The kind young priest walked them both through many difficult, dark days. Molly smiled more, though her fears continued to pursue her.

For a brief time, John continued his work on the docks, taking on jobs from his new clandestine employer after work. Soon, though, Stewart was keeping him busy most days and he stopped showing up for his shift at the docks. He would still leave every morning but when he reached the docklands, he went straight to the bar. Envelopes would be waiting for him most days. Inside the envelope he would find his assignment and payment.

Each assignment consisted of a list of names, addresses, and the amount of money owed by each debtor. On the first day, the list had been delivered by a large man with a thick German accent. His name was Hans. He was a man of few words but he had ways of communicating his intent. His task was to train John. He also would show up if

John ever needed support. He made it clear though, that John should never need support. On their first call, John was to watch what Hans did. Then he would be expected to do it by himself. At the first address, Hans pounded on the door. A woman answered.

"May I help you?" she asked.

"I want Walter Conley."

"Walter, a gentleman is asking for you," she called out.

Walter arrived with a worried look on his face and he motioned for his wife to leave. She backed up a few steps but remained close enough to observe the action.

"You owe twenty-seven dollars," Hans said, looking at the sheet.

"The amount is twenty-five," Walter argued.

Without looking up, Hans slapped the man hard enough to draw blood from his cut upper lip.

"You pay what I say," Hans said.

"I will have the money for you tomorrow," Walter said.

He glanced back at his wife.

"Tomorrow will be thirty dollars," Hans said.

He turned and nodded to John to follow him. They were approaching the next address when John could hold it no longer.

"Why did you have to hit him?"

Hans lowered his eyebrows and scowled at John. Then he shrugged his shoulders and said nothing. At the next house, the man owed fifteen dollars. He quickly paid Hans the money. After counting the money, he punched the man in the stomach. Hans walked away and John followed.

"That was uncalled for. He paid you," John said.

Hans stopped in the middle of the street, forcing buggies and carriages to go around him. He turned and looked at John.

"You want this job or not?"

"I need the money," John said.

It was an honest answer. He needed the money as much as he did not want to do this job. He was faced with a dilemma, and he needed to do what was right. The family needed the money more than he needed to feel good about himself.

"Shut up then," Hans said.

John held his tongue the rest of the day as they collected funds. Some level of violence occurred on almost every visit. They got through half the list.

"Tomorrow you will work the list while I watch," Hans said, then handed John the list and walked away.

The next day it was raining. Hans explained this was good for them because more people would be at home. John did as he was expected to do, which meant that a degree of violence accompanied every transaction. About halfway through the day, John collected a sum owed by a man named Stephen James. He was a small man, very polite, and he quickly paid the amount requested. John turned to leave but Hans remained, glowering first at the little man and then at John. John was several yards from the door when Hans yelled.

"Get back here and finish the job!"

"I have the money," John said quietly.

Hans raised his fist and landed a blow on the top of Stephen James' head. The man gasped, doubled over, then closed his eyes waiting for what might come next.

"I shall not do your job for you again," Hans said.

The threat was palpable.

John said he needed to relieve himself. He found an alley and vomited. He had seen plenty of things in his life, but few as unnecessarily cruel as what he had just witnessed.

Hans told him he was never to visit the restaurant where Stewart had his office. If he needed assistance, Hans could be reached at an address he would give John. A young boy would deliver envelopes to The

Anchor, containing lists and John's salary. John was to place the collected funds in the same envelope for the boy to take to Hans. John had made friends with Clem, the bartender, so he would read the notes to him.

"These names you have, what is this all about?" Clem asked him one day.

"Trust me. You are better off not knowing," John said.

"As long as you don't bring it here. I don't need any more trouble. I appreciate your business, but I don't want to see you do it," Clem said, pointing to the list.

Most of John's work involved small sums of money. Hans handled the big jobs. But one cold day in December, the envelope waiting at The Anchor contained not a list of names, but a single address. John was to show up there just before dark. The money inside was twice what he usually received.

Later that evening, John got there as Hans and a dozen other men arrived. He recognized the type though he didn't recognize the faces. Each man was physically equal to the violent tasks John knew were about to occur. They were in a part of the city he had rarely frequented. Stone mansions and elegant brownstones lined the street. Towering wrought iron street lights illuminated well-kept streets and boulevards. John knew this to be an enclave of wealth and power. For a moment, he thought about the ostentatious Conway mansion in Galway. He'd come halfway across the world but he guessed some things never changed.

Hans was not in charge tonight. The big German was just one of the goons. The man in charge was elegantly dressed, with a well-trimmed beard. He spoke clearly, exuding an authority John knew was not to be questioned.

"An interloper from Boston has had the temerity to threaten our business," he said. "Obviously, this will not be tolerated. Tonight, you men will travel in teams to various locations where the charlatan's henchmen will be found. You will apprehend these men, by whatever means necessary, gag and blindfold them, and bring them here.

As he spoke, a policeman appeared a block away. The tall man walked over to the officer, put an arm around his shoulder, and spoke softly with him. He then reached into his pocket and withdrew an envelope of cash. The officer nodded, took the envelope, and crossed the street to resume walking his beat.

At the appointed hour, the men left in pairs. John was with a man named Herbert. Their quarry was in a pub nearby. Herbert was a more experienced thug, so he would take the lead. He waited behind the saloon while John delivered a note to the man. The ruse worked and a few minutes later the man came around the corner of the pub. Herbert hit him, rendering him momentarily useless. They gagged him, put a sack over his head, and tied his hands behind his back. They marched him back to the appointed meeting place. They were the first to arrive and the tall man seemed pleased.

Seven men were taken captive over the next two hours. The temperature was dropping as they marched the blindfolded captives to an elegant three-story brownstone. The tall man walked up to the door and knocked. Four men were with him at the front entrance, but they remained out of view. A uniformed maid opened the door. Before she could speak, the tall man pushed inside, holding her firmly by the arm as his four ruffians entered the house. John stood with Hans and half a dozen others, guarding the prisoners as the raid proceeded. The intruders collected three small children and their mother. They were brought out into the cold night air in their night clothes. The tall man then grabbed one of the blinded and gagged prisoners—a large, obscenely obese man. He pushed the man toward the house, then jerked the blindfold from his face. The man's eyes bulged when he saw his family being held prisoner.

"Mr. Thomas, you have been warned to cease your business activities in this town, but you have chosen to ignore us. Now look at the situation your unfortunate negligence has created."

The tall man gestured toward the man's terrified wife and children, shivering in the cold.

"Please, please… I will leave town tomorrow. Just do not hurt my family," Thomas said.

"The last time we spoke, you reported our conversation to the police. This cost us a considerable amount of money and bother," the tall man said.

"I will pay, I will leave and never talk to anyone again."

Thomas was pleading now, and he had soiled his clothes.

"Maybe I should cut your tongue out, just to be sure."

The tall man pulled out a long knife and held it close to the man's face.

"No, no, no, please don't…"

The man's wife struggled in vain to free herself from the grip of a goon who was holding her.

"What can I do?" Thomas asked.

"Are you ready to negotiate in good faith, or do I need to have your family watch as I burn your house to the ground?"

"I will give you whatever you want," Thomas said.

The tall man smiled as one of his goons slit the man's throat.

John made his way home much later that night, filled with guilt and shame. He had become a part of the kind of thing his family had always despised. He did not want to face his mother. Nelly had always looked up to him. What if she found out what he had done? What would Mickey Delaney have said? He thought about how his brothers and father had died, and he wept as he walked the dark city streets on his way home. He slept a few hours and left before his sister and mother awakened. They had come to America for a fresh start. He'd never thought it would be this.

The following morning, Molly and Nelly arrived at the factory as it began to snow. It was bitterly cold and they were almost frostbitten by the time they reached the front door. Inside, a dozen other workers were helping to bring one of the cobblers downstairs. Ralph, the cobbler Molly had been assisting, was moaning and his breathing was shallow.

"Out of the way everyone, give him some air, " said Quigley.

Molly hurried to Ralph's side, felt for a pulse, and urged Quigley to get a doctor, but it was too late. The cobbler breathed his last in her arms.

There was pandemonium on the floor as the other cobblers and assistants realized their friend and co-worker was dead. Quigley seemed unsure about what to do next.

"You might want to tell everyone they should go back to their work," Molly whispered. "Tell them that's what Ralph would have wanted."

Quigley considered her advice and quickly took it.

She waited with Ralph's body until the undertaker arrived, then climbed the stairs to the third floor, where they had worked together. She sat down at the workbench, not sure what would come next. Without Ralph, she knew her job would be in jeopardy. Absently, she began to finger the pieces of leather they had cut and were ready to begin sewing. Almost without thinking, she began to stitch the way Ralph had shown her, pushing the needle through the layers with a sure, practiced hand. As she shaped the pieces on the iron last, a boot gradually took form. Molly wept as she sewed—for Ralph, a good man who had been kind to her, for her dwindling prospects at the factory, and for John, for whatever he was now doing when he left in the morning. She knew he wasn't working at the docks anymore.

The cobbler at the next workbench had observed Molly's work and had offered suggestions on some of the more difficult parts of the construction. Molly learned quickly and by the end of the workday, she had a pair of leather boots well underway. She had not heard from Quigley since early that morning and she dreaded what might await her when she did.

Just then, the man came up the stairs.

"Molly Delaney, I'm afraid I'm going to have to let you…"

He stopped in mid-sentence. He stared at the boots, then back at Molly. He came closer to examine the work, carefully inspecting the stitching.

Suddenly, he found his voice.

"Those boots are to be delivered no later than Friday. Will you be able to finish them in time?"

Molly nodded, not trusting her voice.

"Fine. You're promoted to cobbler. I'll give you a two-dollar-a-week raise. But you'll need to work six days a week now through Christmas, just like all the other cobblers.

Quigley left without waiting for an answer.

It was already dark by the time Molly and Nelly bundled up for the freezing walk home. Nelly was full of questions but Molly was emotionally exhausted by the events of the day.

"Mam, two dollars more a week! We'll have enough for a proper Christmas dinner!"

Molly forced a smile for Nelly's sake, though Christmas dinner was the last thing on her mind. Her good fortune today had come at the expense of human life, and that robbed her of much of the satisfaction—and the relief—she should have felt.

"Let's just get home, Nelly. We can think about all that later. For now, all I want is a cup of tea and bed."

Nelly hugged her mother, blissfully unaware of the true state of Molly's heart.

The following Sunday, Molly sent Nelly to Mass alone. John had left before either of them were awake.

"There is something I must do today," Molly said. "Please give Father Matthew my best regards when you see him."

Nelly was curious, but not unduly concerned. Her mother knew best—she was sure of that—and if she had something to do, it must be important.

Molly waited for Nelly to leave, then dressed and went downstairs. An uncomfortable silence settled over the tavern as she walked in. She looked around, then noticed a table of young men—some of them Irish.

"I'm looking for my son, John. There's been an accident. It's important that I find him at once," she said, mixing truth with fiction.

Her deception had been successful. A red-haired man at the table motioned to her.

"I can help you find him, ma'am."

As Molly learned bits and pieces of the truth from John's friend, she kept her expression neutral. The situation might be every bit as bad as she had feared, but she had no time for her emotions. Armed with the address of the saloon where John was likely to be found, she set out for the docklands. The wind was blowing, and the chill reminded her of the winter winds off the Atlantic on the Irish Coast. She stopped several times to take shelter from the wind between buildings or within doorways. When she finally reached The Anchor after hours in a fight against the elements, she was exhausted, but she repeated her ruse, this time addressing her concern to Clem, the bartender. The man promptly escorted her to a partially obscured corner where she found John behind a small desk.

His blood ran cold when he saw her.

"Mam, how did you… I mean, why are you here?"

His work had made him callous and uncaring, but not yet callous enough for this confrontation with his mother.

"John, I have walked for hours in the freezing cold to find you. My heart is broken over what it seems you have become, but we don't have time for that now."

"Mam, I… I mean everything I did… I did this for us, we needed the money."

Molly's eyes were hard and cold. She slapped him hard across the face.

"Don't lie to me and don't lie to yourself. We both know why you've taken up this shameful life. You're just like your father. He loved the violence and the power, and so do you. But at least he was fighting for the right reason. You… you're no better than the filthy Tans."

John's face stung, but that wasn't the worst of it. He looked at the floor, unable to meet her gaze.

"This stops today. I don't care if we live on porridge every meal for the rest of our lives, John. No Delaney has ever exchanged his soul for money, and it's not going to start now."

"Mam, I don't think I can get out of this."

John's admission broke her heart. She moved her chair closer to his, pulling his head down on her shoulder. She whispered in his ear.

"Tell me everything, son."

He didn't stop talking until the tale was through. She sat for a moment and thought about it. She asked him several questions about some of the details of his arrangement.

"I'll need an envelope, pen, and paper," she said.

John provided these and then sat watching as she wrote. After she finished, she asked him for all the money he had with him. He handed her forty-five dollars. She kept five and put the rest in the envelope with the note. As she sealed the envelope, a runner came in with a message for John.

"Please wait, young man," she said.

She read the note, then handed her envelope to the boy.

"Get this to your boss as fast as you can."

She looked at John and shook her head, then tore up the note from Stewart.

"Let's go, John. We're going to pay for a carriage. I don't think I can face the cold again today."

John raised an eyebrow.

"Didn't I tell you? I'm now a cobbler, not just an assistant. It pays well, though it's no gold mine. But we can afford the occasional carriage."

Molly was full of surprises today, John thought. He was realizing for the first time that she was no less resilient than his father had been.

"What did you write in the letter?" he asked.

"The letter was from you. You thanked Mr. Stewart for the opportunities he's given you but let him know that a family emergency had called you away. You assured him of your ongoing discretion. And you returned most of the money."

"I will have to steer clear of anyone who might recognize me for a while."

"That would probably be wise."

"Do you think Mr. Lewis might help me get my old job back?"

"Perhaps, if you go to him with the proper amount of humility."

John fell silent.

"Oh, and there's the matter of Nelly," she said.

"Nelly? What's happened? Is she safe?"

"She's hurt, John. You've been her best friend for as long as she can remember, but now you're a stranger. You're never home and when you are, you ignore her. Your sister's heart is broken."

John wept for the first time since Elizabeth's death.

"You can change that, starting today. Starting the moment we get there. You hug your sister as soon as you go through that door, and you tell her you love her and that you're sorry. Then you live up to that every day from now on. No exceptions."

John grinned through his tears.

"Anyone ever tell you you're a Delaney through and through?" he asked.

"You're just noticing that?"

Molly grinned and tousled her son's hair.

"Time to find our way home again," she said.

ACKNOWLEDGMENTS

I must begin by thanking my LORD and Savior Jesus Christ. Without his loving care and guidance, nothing would be possible for me. I rely upon him daily and would be totally a wreck without his love. Next, I'd like to thank my family. My wife Terry Beeson, daughter Nicole Mayfield, son-in-law John Mayfield, and my grandchildren Claire, Jacob, and Bella Mayfield have all been my guide. The unending love they show me has been like a beacon light shining brightly that guides a wondering ship to safety. Thank you to so many of you that read my first book and gave me encouragement. My dear friend Doug Troxel for taking the time to correct all my many written flaws. Denise Hewitt Long, an incredibly talented wordsmith put her own needs aside to help me with this book. It is a rare thing to have a friend for over 55 years that you can count on. Denise is that friend. Thanks to my dear friend Susan Chambers for editing this book. She is an unusually wise person that can take the ramblings of a common storyteller and make them a work of art. Thank you Robert Henry of Right Hand Publishing for guiding me through the publishing maze. And finally, thanks to Robin Locke Monda of Locke Monda Graphic Arts for the incredible cover design work.